Eve Bunting

Sixth-Grade Sleepover

Everyone in the sixth-grade reading club will be going to the sleepover in the cafeteria—everyone except Janey. And that's because she has a horribly embarrassing secret problem. Even Rosie, the weird new girl, will be there, and Pebbles, the class rabbit, and all the boys in the reading club, including Blake Conway, the cutest guy in the whole sixth grade.

Sylvie Pedersen will be wearing her darling new pink pj's. Janey is almost positive Sylvie likes Blake. Worse, she's almost positive Blake likes Sylvie.

"I'll be there and I'll help you," her friend Claudia says.

But Janey knows nothing can help. Until she thinks of *the plan*.

The plan will make everything possible.

Unfortunately, plans can go wrong. And on the night of the sixth-grade sleepover Janey discovers that some secrets are better shared, that big problems become bigger if you keep them hidden, and that a boy doesn't always do what you think he'll do . . . or a rabbit either!

Sixth-Grade
Sleepover

Also by Eve Bunting

Harcourt

Brace

Jovanovich

Publishers

San Diego   New York   London

Eve Bunting

Sixth-Grade Sleepover

Requests for permission to make copies of
any part of the work should be mailed to:
Permissions, Harcourt Brace Jovanovich, Publishers,
Orlando, Florida 32887.

Library of Congress Cataloging-in-Publication Data

Bunting, Eve, 1928–
   Sixth-Grade sleepover.

   Summary: Janey worries that the sixth-grade
Rabbit Reading Club's all-night sleepover
will expose her fear of the dark,
but it turns out that she is not
the only member with a secret.
   [1. Fear—Fiction. 2. Reading—Fiction.
3. Schools—Fiction] I. Title.
PZ7.B91527Si 1986   [Fic]   86-4679
ISBN 0-15-275350-8

Designed by Michael Farmer

Printed in the United States of America

   C D E

With thanks to
Lara Clardy and Vicki Waller,
special teachers of
special students

Sixth-Grade
Sleepover

1

My friend Claudia and I are both Rabbits. Not real ones, of course, though we do have a real rabbit in our classroom. His name is Pebbles, and he's our mascot. We were going to call him Junior, but the very first day we got him he kept running across the floor and leaving these little black droppings.

"Look! Pebbles!" Jefferson Ames yelled. Jefferson is our sixth-grade clown.

So that's how Pebbles got his name. Now he's paper-trained, and his pebbles are all in one place.

Claudia and I are in the Rabbit Reading Club at Fred Barrington Elementary. When we meet each other, or another club member, we instantly give the secret Bunny Sign. That's Rabbit Rule Number 4 of our *Grass Roots Rabbit Handbook*. To give the Bunny Sign, you spread apart the two fingers of your left hand and hold them behind your head so they stick up like rabbit ears or like an Indian with two feathers in his hair. We definitely do not give the sign to non-Rabbits (Rule Number 5).

So this morning, when Claudia and I were on our way to our first class, we were stunned when Rosie Green, the new girl, gave the secret Bunny Sign to us.

"Did you see what I saw?" Claudia gasped when we were past. "How did *she* get to be a Rabbit? She's too new!"

"Maybe it wasn't the sign," I said. "Maybe she was just— just waving."

Claudia shook her head. "It was it!"

I was truly astounded. "She must have proved herself to Mr. Puttinski then." Mr. Puttinski is our sixth-grade teacher. "Putt-Putt would never let an unqualified person into the club," I added. "He knows we have our reputations to think about."

"Maybe he'll tell us this morning, then," Claudia said. "He ought to make some kind of announcement. He can't just ask *any* strange person . . ." She stopped, but I knew what she was thinking, though she didn't say it.

The new girl, Rosie Green, is a *very* strange person. First, she looks strange. She has a little tiny face and pointy chin, and she wears the weirdest clothes, with the sleeves too short on her sweaters and the legs too short on her pants. And then she has these big, skinny feet. I swear, Rosie Green's feet are the biggest I've ever seen. I think they're longer than my dad's.

Also, Rosie Green acts strange. We all like to hold Pebbles because he's so soft and warm. But Rosie wants to hold him all the time, petting him, whispering stuff to him. Mr. Puttinski has to pry her and Pebbles apart at lunchtime. Once Claudia saw Rosie cry when Putt-Putt took Pebbles off her lap.

Not that you have to be super normal, or have small feet,

or look great like Sylvie Pedersen to be in the Rabbit Club. If you did, Claudia and I might never have made it. For the looks part, I mean. You just have to be a person who loves reading and who has read a certain number of books and done book reports on them. R-A-B-B-I-T-S stand for "Read-A-Book: Bring-It-To-School." Mr. Puttinski and Mrs. Golden, our reading specialist, started it up.

"Maybe Putt-Putt decided . . ." I began, and then I went "Oh oh" and stopped. Blake Conway and Malcolm Price had just appeared around the corner by the bathrooms.

"Oh oh," I said again, and my heart was going flip-flop, the way it does when Blake Conway appears from any-where. I think he is the nicest boy in the whole sixth grade, though Claudia thinks Malcolm is. Luckily, they are both Rabbits.

"What do we do?" I whispered.

It's not easy to give the Bunny Sign to boy Rabbits. Boys are strange. You don't know what they're thinking or what to expect. Sometimes a boy speaks to you when he meets you, and sometimes he doesn't. Sometimes he acts as if he knows you really well, and the next time it's as if he's never seen you before in his whole life.

Actually, I find boys one of the great mysteries of life. I think it's because I don't have any brothers, just two sisters. Claudia has a brother, and she says that isn't any help at all. Boys are a mystery to her, too.

Which makes it difficult to follow Rabbit Rule Number 4 when meeting a boy Rabbit. To give the secret sign or not to give the secret sign? Suppose you do, and he looks at you as if you're Loony Tunes? The thing to do is pretend to scratch your head and hope he doesn't go, "O-oo, dan-druff!"

We were only a few steps apart now, and I swept a secret

glance in Blake's direction. My glance was sufficiently sweeping to take in his nice blue-checked shirt, his blue eyes, his hair that's kind of mousy brown. Except that nothing about Blake could ever be mousy. You could probably describe his hair as dark blond. The end of my sweeping glance told me that he was looking right at me and that he was waggling his fingers behind his head. Malcolm was, too.

"Hi," I said, signing like mad.

"Hi," Claudia echoed. Claudia and I echo each other a lot.

"Have you seen this?" Blake set a piece of yellow paper on top of my pile of books. I tried to lift it, and everything began to slip.

Oh, crumbs! I could just see my books slither helter-skelter on the floor, see my sixth-grade reader flutter open and the picture of Blake that I'd cut from last year's class pictures slide out, and see Blake pick it up and *know*! I squirmed desperately and managed to save the books, but the sheet of yellow paper wafted down the hall.

Claudia gave me a despairing look.

Blake brought the paper back. "I'll hold it for you," he said.

In big black letters across the top of the yellow page it said:

SIXTH-GRADE SLEEPOVER
FOR RABBITS ONLY

All Rabbits are invited to a marathon reading sleepover on Friday night, March 14. Activities will begin at 6:00 P.M. and end with breakfast Saturday morning 9:00 A.M.

It's going to be FUN. There'll be lots of reading, games, and music.

Parent permission slips and more information will be given to interested Rabbits in Mr. Puttinski's class.

Claudia and I exchanged glances. We've been exchanging glances for so long that we don't have to speak a word to know what the other is thinking.

I gulped.

"We're going to be there *all night*?" Claudia asked at last. "Boy Rabbits and girl Rabbits both?"

Blake folded the paper small and slid it in the pocket of his checked shirt. "I guess," he said. "Us, and Putt-Putt, and Goldie. We'll probably find out more in class."

It was the total most Blake had ever said to me at one time. I was overcome.

"Do you two young girl Rabbits plan on going?" Malcolm asked. That's the way Malcolm talks, as if he's an adult and the rest of us are kids. It's kind of funny. Blake is more ordinary. I guess I like ordinary better.

"I suppose we'll be going." Claudia's really good at being cool when she remembers.

Malcolm pushed back his baseball cap. He has curly black hair that sticks out on the sides, and he always wears that Dodger cap. Once I told Claudia I thought he was probably bald on top, and she turned pale and screamed.

"Well, see you," Malcolm said.

"OK." Claudia and I walked on in a daze.

"A sleepover," she breathed, not cool at all now. "Us and those cute boy Rabbits. Reading books and playing games and listening to music. What kinds of *games* do you think we'll have?"

I was speechless.

"And we get to have *breakfast* with them the next morning." Claudia stared at me, big-eyed. "*Us*, having breakfast with Malcolm Price and Blake Conway."

I notice she always puts Malcolm's name first when she talks about him and Blake, which is probably natural.

"There'll be us and ten or twelve other Rabbits," I said. Sometimes Claudia gets carried away.

"Us sleeping in our sleeping bags, under the same roof . . ."

"It's scary, all right," I said.

Scary! Suddenly I remembered. "Oh, Claudia! What will I do? I'll never be able to go. If I do, everyone will find out about my problem. Blake will know and . . ."

"Hey, wait a sec, Janey! Calm down! You *can* go. I'll help. It'll be OK."

I was shaking my head, harder and harder.

"You mean you're going to miss out on all of that? Just because you're . . ."

"Sh!" I interrupted her. "Don't you dare say it, Claudia Fairfield. Nobody in the world knows except you, and your parents, and me and my parents, and . . ." I could have added "Doctor Bishop," but I didn't want to get into that. "Anyway, don't ever mention it out loud except when we're by ourselves. And not even then."

"Oh, Janey, honestly! It's not that awful. And it won't be half as good if you don't come."

"Sure it will. Marvelous Malcolm will be there." I grinned at her and tried to look as if it didn't really matter, which wasn't easy since it mattered a whole bunch.

2

"Unless, between now and then, you can get rid of the problem," Claudia said.

We were lying on my bed, after school, reading the handouts Putt-Putt had given us.

"Oh sure," I said semisarcastically. "I've just had it for about eleven years. I'm sure I'm going to snap out of it in one week. I mean, if it was *that* easy, don't you think I'd have done it before now? Anyway, I don't want to talk about it. I'm just not going to the sleepover."

"OK, OK." Claudia waved some of Putt-Putt's stuff over her head and began nonchalantly to read from it.

I lay back on the pillows, just as nonchalantly, and closed my eyes. I wasn't fooling Claudia one bit. She knew I was hearing every word. And she wasn't fooling me. I knew she was reading out all the best parts, *tempting* me to go, no matter what.

" 'Dear Rabbits,' " Claudia read. " 'Let me tell you more about the Rabbit sleepover.

" '(1) Each Rabbit will eat a meal before he/she comes at around 6:00 P.M.

" '(2) Each Rabbit will bring a healthy snack for later. Don't forget . . . rabbits love carrots and apples. BUT DON'T FEED THE RABBIT LETTUCE!' "

Claudia grinned over at me. "Don't feed the rabbit lettuce!" is our room joke. We take it in turn to look after Pebbles. As soon as you go near the cage, everyone bellows, "Don't feed the rabbit lettuce!" We did, early on, before we knew Pebbles's eating habits. Believe me, lettuce does *not* agree with that little rabbit. What *he* did after that lettuce is just too gross to be mentionable.

"Will I keep on reading?" Claudia asked. "Or since you're not going, maybe you're not interested?"

"Oh, keep on if you like," I said.

" '(3) Bring a sleeping bag.

" '(4) Bring books, books, books. For reading, reading, reading.

" '(5) Bring pj's, a nightshirt, long johns, or other sleeping apparel of your choice. Also toothbrushes. (And don't give me this bit about rabbits not having to brush their teeth.)' "

Claudia dropped the pink sheet of paper as if it had suddenly become too hot to handle. " 'Bring pj's'! Is he kidding? All I'm taking off are my *shoes*. I'm not wearing pj's. Are you, Janey?"

"Remember? I'm not going."

"Oh, yeah. I forgot." Claudia blew her bangs out of her eyes. Her hair is so short that when she blows like that, every single piece of hair lifts and resettles. "I bet *nobody* wears pj's. Can you imagine? Letting the *boys* see you like that?"

8

This was a truly fascinating subject. I'd forgotten that I wasn't interested. "And seeing *them!*" I said. "How embarrassing!" I rolled onto my stomach and buried my face in my pillow.

The papers from Putt-Putt were all different colors. I sat up, took a green one, and looked at it, humming a little to show how unimportant it all was, but inside I was thinking, "There has to be *some* way. *Some* way." The more I read and the more Claudia and I talked, the more I wanted to go.

"TO BE A QUALIFYING RABBIT," I read.

"(1) Turn in this month's book reports, signed by at least one parent. (400 pages minimum, Rabbits. Goldie and Putt-Putt will *not* be conned.)

"(2) Return the Parent Contract (blue page).

"(3) If you have any special medical problems, make sure your parents talk to us about them."

Underneath, in capital letters, it said, "ONLY ONE RABBIT IS EXCUSED FROM BOOK REPORTS AND PARENT CONSENT FORMS— PEBBLES."

Claudia had been reading the same green sheet at the same time.

"Janey, why don't you just have your mom tell Goldie or Silly Putty *your* medical problem," she said. "Nobody else needs to know. They're both safe. Goldie could probably fix it for you if she understood."

I bounced on the bed. "I will not tell anyone. Truly, Claudia, there are times when you are so insensitive."

Claudia looked offended. "I'm just giving advice."

Downstairs the phone rang, and I heard my littlest sister, Oriana, answer it in her high, pipey voice. She's not supposed to because she sounds really rude on the phone, and we haven't managed to train her yet.

"Who's there?" she yelled, and then I heard my big little

sister, Rachel, who's six, trying to pull the phone from her and hissing, "You're not *allowed*. Give it to me."

Thank goodness no boys ever call me. I mean, how embarrassing!

"It's for you, Janey," Rachel called. "It's only a girl."

I rolled my eyes and slid off the bed. "Would you believe Rachel's supposed to be *better* than Oriana?"

I didn't hurry down the stairs. Face it, if it *had* been a boy, especially *that* boy, I'd have been down in a flash.

"Hello?" I said.

"Is this Jane?"

"Yes." Hardly anyone calls me Jane, though I'd like it if they would.

"This is Rosie Green." Pause, pause. "I don't know if you know me. I've only been at Barrington for . . ."

"Sure I know you. I think I've talked to you a couple of times."

More pause. "You told me not to feed the rabbit lettuce."

I must have said more than *that*. Anyway. "Oh. Well, I *do* know you're in the Rabbit Club."

"Yes."

I waited, picturing Rosie on the other end. Why was she calling me?

"It's about the sleepover," Rosie said. "I really want to go. But my mom works from four till midnight on Fridays, and I have no way to get to school. She said if I could find someone to drive me there, she'd do the pickup in the morning . . . so I was wondering if your mom could give me a ride there, then my mom . . ."

I interrupted again. "The thing is, I don't think I'm going. I'll ask Claudia for you, if you like. Claudia Fairfield. She's a Rabbit, too."

"I know. She's talked to me. She told me not to feed the

rabbit lettuce, same as you did." More pause. *Honestly!* I thought. *Is that really all Claudia and I ever said to her? It wouldn't have hurt us to be a bit friendlier!*

"How come you're not going?" Rosie asked.

"I just can't."

Oriana and Rachel came running through the hallway. "I'm going to *kill* you, Rachel," Oriana yelled as they raced up the stairs.

"Anyway, congratulations on getting to be a Rabbit," I said into the phone.

"Thanks."

"You sure must have spent all your time since you got here reading books."

"Yeah."

"Wasn't it hard to get all the reports to Goldie on time? And this month's 400 pages?"

"She didn't make me write everything out. I just had to tell her what the stories were about, and she asked me some questions. It's because I'm new, and I didn't get started as quickly as the rest of you."

"Wow! Lucky!" I said. "The reading part's fun. I don't like writing the reports so much." Upstairs I could hear Claudia screaming, too. "Oriana, you are *not* allowed to throw water." There was more shrieking.

"My mom signed the forms that said I'd really read the books, so that was OK," Rosie said on the phone.

"Great!" I'd run out of conversation.

Now Rachel was standing beside me, looking like a drowned mouse. "I'm going to tell Mom. Oriana's going to get it for throwing water. You're going to get it, too. You're supposed to be watching us."

"Get a towel and dry off, dumbo," I said. "It's just my little sister," I explained into the phone. "She's having problems, so I'd better go. Oh, where do you live? I'll tell Claudia."

"Over on Hillcrest. The apartment building on the corner. The one's that's just been built."

I knew the place. It looked like a great blank box. But that wasn't why my heart was doing its flip-flops. "Hillcrest?" I asked. And then I added, very casually, "One of the boys from school lives on that street. In fact, if you're in that apartment building, he's . . ."

"Right next door. Blake Conway. I know. I bet his parents were mad when they put up those awful, ugly apartments. I *could* ask *him*," Rosie was saying, "but he's a boy, and it's hard to ask boys things. Maybe not for you, but for me."

"It's hard for me, too," I managed.

"Maybe I could get my mom to ask his mom. They've met, I know. But it would be better if I could go with one of the girls, and I wasn't sure . . ."

"Uh, well, just wait. I'm sure it'll be OK to ride with Claudia. She can tell you tomorrow."

"OK. Thanks."

I hung up the phone and stood staring at it. Rosie Green, weird Rosie Green, lived next door to Blake Conway. And her mother knew his mother. I was totally overcome.

3

I rushed up the stairs and leaned against the inside of my bedroom door, ignoring Rachel, who was pounding on it behind me. "Guess what?" I gasped, and I told Claudia about Rosie's call and watched her eyes get wide. Claudia can make her eyes extremely big, which is why her brother sometimes calls her Claudia Frisbee Face.

Claudia could hardly believe the fact of Rosie's living next door to Blake. And all the possible possibilities. Before we knew it, it was four-thirty and Dad was home. Dad works for an insurance company and usually gets in about an hour before Mom. I asked him if it was OK for Claudia to stay and eat with us as we had some very important matters to ponder, and he said sure. So she called *her* dad, who is an artist and home all the time. He said OK, too.

Mom had left chicken to defrost this morning, and Dad fixed it with mushroom soup and cheese, which is one of his specialties. Claudia and I made the salad. Then Mom came home, and we ate, and Mom told Oriana that she shouldn't throw water, and then she told Rachel that she shouldn't be such a tell-tale, that a little water never hurt anyone, and that it had made her hair curl up so prettily.

"Frizzed!" I muttered, but fortunately only Claudia heard me.

I'd warned Claudia not to say anything about the sleep-over as I needed time to think, and she didn't. Claudia is very trustworthy.

After dinner I asked if we could be excused to go back to my room.

"Certainly," Mom said. "You and Claudia and Rachel and Oriana may *all* be excused."

"And after you've done the dishes you may *all* go to your rooms." Dad smiled smugly. My dad never misses a trick.

When we'd cleared everything away, Claudia and I went upstairs, and I warned Oriana and Rachel not to disturb us on pain of sudden death. Dad had brought them home new stickers, so they wanted to go put them in their sticker albums anyway.

Claudia and I put on a Bruce Springsteen record and lay on my bed again for further discussion.

"It's a good thing Rosie Green isn't gorgeous," Claudia said. "Like Sylvie Pedersen." She knows I worry about Sylvie Pedersen because Sylvie is so cute and I think she likes Blake. I have definite suspicions.

"I wouldn't care." I pedaled my legs in the air.

"Yes, you would. But maybe Rosie will get to be good friends with Blake, and he'll like her a lot even if she is weird." Claudia considered this. "Maybe we ought to get to be real good friends with Rosie, too."

I didn't like the way that sounded, as if the only reason for being friends with someone was because she lived next to a boy you liked. "We would be anyway, now that she's a Rabbit," I said, which was true but didn't make me feel a whole lot better.

Claudia started pedaling beside me. "You know, your problem's not *that* bad," she said. "It's not as if you sleep-walk, and you'd have to worry that you'd sleep-walk over to Blake and bend down and *kiss* him. . . ."

"Crumbs!" I fell over and lay gasping. "Don't *say* that."

"Or suppose you *talked* in your sleep, and you said, 'I love Blake Conway . . . I love Blake Conway'? And everybody would hear!"

I groaned. "I'd *die*! And everyone would ask, 'Who's that talking?' And I'd wake up and I'd say, 'It's Claudia Fairfield. But she made a mistake. *She* loves Malcolm Price.' Bald Malcolm Price, because he'll have his cap off, and he'll be bald as a Ping-Pong ball."

Of course, my two little sisters had to come in to see what was going on, and I threw my slippers at them.

When they'd ducked out, Claudia said, "And since you don't walk or talk or even *snore*, pretty please, Janey, do come."

"I don't think I can," I said, and suddenly I didn't feel like laughing anymore because I'd picked up that pink sheet of paper again. And there, plain as plain, it said, "(6) Lights out, 12 Midnight."

Dad and Jock and I walked Claudia home. Jock is our fat orange cat who spends nine-tenths of his life sleeping in a big flowerpot on the porch. Actually, Claudia only lives across the street from us, so it's no big deal. But we're not allowed to go alone after five o'clock. I wouldn't want to anyway.

We waited till she was safely inside her house, and then

Dad and Jock and I decided to go all the way around the block.

I guess I was quieter than I usually am, and it wasn't long before Dad sensed something was wrong. He's good at sensing things.

"Want to talk?" He swung my hand in his. Under the bright lamplight I could see our shadows, one tall, one short, one squat and shapeless. The squat, shapeless one was Jock, not me.

So I told Dad about the sleepover and about how much I wanted to go, but I didn't tell about Blake Conway because, well, Dad doesn't quite know I like boys yet. I don't *think* he knows.

"Will it be all night?" he asked.

I nodded. "Starts at 6 P.M. and ends at 9 A.M."

A dog came on the bark from a front yard to rush at Jock, but Jock hissed him away. Jock could hiss away the Wolves of Willoughby Chase.

"You know what, honey-bun?" Dad said. "You may be worrying for nothing. Maybe they keep the cafeteria lights on all night. I would, with a bunch of kids around."

"Uh-uh." I shook my head. "It was right there in the Rabbit sheets that Putt-Putt gave us: 'Lights out, 12 Midnight.' It's going to be darker than dark in that old cafeteria." I swallowed. Even under the bright yellow glow from the streetlights, even with Dad's hand covering mine, keeping me warm and safe, and Jock purring like a steam engine around my feet, I'd begun to shiver. The very thought of the dark does that to me every time.

4

Mom is a personnel manager with Rombergs, a big company with its head offices here in Pasadena, California. It took me a long time to learn how to spell personnel: two n's, one l. It took me longer to know what it meant, and I'm still not sure. She hires the people who work for Rombergs, and when they do a bad job, she has to fire them, so that part's a bummer.

Mom is super, super careful about anybody she has in to look after us. And that's because it was a baby-sitter she had for me when I was little who gave me my "problem." "Night terrors" is what Dr. Bishop called it, which really means imagining all sorts of awful things lurking in the dark.

The baby-sitter's name was Mrs. McCormack, and Mom says, "A nicer wee body you'd never hope to meet." Mom was born in Scotland, and she still has a few of her Scottish sayings.

Well, Mrs. McCormack wasn't as nice a wee body as she seemed to be. If I was "bad," she closed me in the hall closet and locked the door. Now that I'm older, I don't know why I never told. Maybe at the time I was too scared. If Mrs. McCormack knew I'd told, she'd have kept me in the closet forever. I was too scared. All Mom and Dad knew was that I began screaming at night when they'd turn off the lights.

When my parents found out what was going on, Mom said she thought Dad was "going to tear the woman apart, limb from limb. And her standing there saying, 'It was just discipline, sir. My own mother disciplined me that way, and I turned out to be perfectly fine.' "

"You turned out to be a monster," Dad shouted.

Of course, I don't remember any of that. The dark closet I remember perfectly. I had to draw the inside of it for Dr. Bishop, and draw my feelings, and talk about how I hadn't "deserved" to be shut in there, that I hadn't been bad at all. I guess I went to Dr. Bishop the year I was eight. I hated it. It was like being back in that closet all over again. I kept crying and begging Mom and Dad to let me stop, and Mom cried, too, and told Dad they shouldn't force me to go. And when I left, Dr. Bishop said he was disappointed that he hadn't been able to help me more and that they should bring me back when I was ready. He also said that until then he didn't see anything wrong with my sleeping regularly with a light. All the time I was seeing him, I was afraid he was going to make me spend a whole night in the dark, or something awful like that, to get me over it. So I was really relieved. I was so relieved that I almost said I'd stay with him some more, but I didn't.

Our house has night lights everywhere, the kind that plug into wall outlets. Mom says she's glad because it's safer for the little girls, who could bump into something or trip on the stairs on the way to the bathroom—which doesn't make sense because Rachel and Oriana's bathroom is attached to their room. But it's Mom's way of making me feel all those lights aren't only for me.

The two pink lamps with their frilly shades that stand on my dresser burn all night long. I used to make myself wake up about every hour to make sure they were still on. Now I know they always are. I know I'm never in the dark. When I sleep over at Claudia's, we keep the lights on, too. Once there was a power failure and I woke up, and all around me was blacker than black. I guess I nearly brought their house down screaming, and Claudia's mom had to call my parents. And Claudia's brother, Dan, said, "Is she having an attack, or what?" But mostly I stay safe.

The morning after Claudia and I'd discussed the sleepover, I lay in bed listening to Mom shower. She leaves before Dad. Last night I'd stuffed all of Putt-Putt's papers into my wastebasket and promised myself to forget them. The different colors fanned out like a rainbow, and they were so tempting that I couldn't stand it. So after a few seconds I hopped out of bed, grabbed the papers, and hopped back. If only . . . if only. . . .

"You're twelve years old, Jane Winston," I said out loud. "Is it worth it to you to miss all this fun just because you're a big baby, afraid of the dark?"

"Knock knock," Mom called out, coming into my room in her yellow bathrobe. The blue towel wrapped around her wet hair was paler than the blue of her eyes. The only one of us who looks like Mom is Oriana. She has the same blond hair and dimples. Rachel and I both got Dad's reddish brown, crimpy hair, though we have more of it than he does. We also got his gray-green eyes and pale eyelashes. Better for us than for him, though, as Dad keeps reminding us. When we get older, we can use mascara. Men are not much into makeup yet, at least not any of the ones I know.

Mom sat on the edge of my bed and picked up one of the papers. "You'd really like to go to this, wouldn't you, Janey?"

I nodded and nibbled on the ribbon at the neck of my nightgown. It had that salty, chewed-on-before taste.

"How about if I speak to Mrs. Golden?" Mom asked.

I spat out the ribbon. "Uh-uh. Double uh-uh. Triple . . ."

Mom put a finger across my lips. "Wait, honey. Wait. Dad and I talked this over endlessly last night. We decided one of us should call Goldie and check out how it's going to be. We'd do that anyway before we'd allow you to go. It would be perfectly natural. And we could ask her, casually, if the lights will be on or off."

"Off," I said, tapping the papers on the bed.

" 'Lights out' might only mean it's time for all of you to settle down and go to sleep. When I was in boarding school . . ." She stopped and smiled at me, but for once I didn't smile back. When Mom starts a sentence that way, we all wink at each other because it's usually the start of a horror story. "When I was in boarding school, we had to eat everything on our plates. Once I was in the sick room, and there was this awful gray-looking sausage on my plate. I put it inside my hot-water bottle so I could drop it down the toilet later. But the sausage wouldn't come out! And it began to *stink!*" Mom had millions of stories about boarding school, but this morning nothing she could have said would have been funny.

She pleated the top of my bed cover. "We had 'Lights out' at nine-thirty every night. But that only meant the big light overhead. We always had small ones above the doors and along the corridors."

"Fred Barrington Elementary isn't a boarding school,

Mom. Kids don't usually sleep over. They don't *need* lights above the doors or along the corridors."

"Well, maybe they'll have to get some. Kids will still need to go to the bathroom."

"It'll be all dark and . . ." I could feel myself getting teary, and then Mom took my hand, and her face twisted up, too, and she said, "Oh shoot!"

Mom feels guilty about my problem and about Mrs. McCormack, though I've told her a thousand times it wasn't *her* fault. But sometimes, secretly, I think it was, just a bit, for having Mrs. McCormack and trusting her. Then I hate myself.

"Will you let me try to find out, Janey?" Mom asked softly.

I lay, chewing on my ribbon. "Promise you won't even *hint*."

"I promise. Would I hint without your permission?" She stroked back my hair. "I think I maybe can convince Goldie. . . ."

I sat up. "You'll give it away."

"No I won't. I am the soul of discretion."

I lay down again.

"You know, honey, I don't like this cover-up stuff. You hide from something, and it grows and gets worse. It's so much better to face it—to ask for help."

I turned my face away, and I heard Mom sigh as she rose to leave. Since it was daylight, she clicked off the two pink lamps on my dresser as she went past.

I was still in bed when Claudia called to check what we should wear to school, and I couldn't help telling her that I *might* be able to go to the sleepover after all. I told her Mom was going to try to find out how it would be and maybe make some subtle suggestions.

"Your mom is *very* subtle," Claudia said. "And anyway,

I've been thinking about it, and I'm sure they won't leave us in total darkness. I mean, who *knows* what those boys would get up to?"

Nothing, of course. But sometimes Claudia and I talk as if we're in danger of immediate romantic attack.

When we were walking to school, she said, "Want to ask Rosie Green to eat lunch with us today?"

"Sure." We didn't look at each other, probably because we were both feeling a bit ashamed. Then Claudia said, "And I got the best idea last night. Now, since you're going for sure, it will be absolutely perfect."

"Wait. I'm not going for sure."

Claudia paid no attention. "What I'm going to say to Rosie is that my mom will drive. I've already checked. Then I'll say it would be great if *her* mom picked us up. And since Rosie lives next door to Blake Conway, it would be silly for us not to take him, too, and bring him back. We'd save on gas. . . ."

"And save our parents' time," I added piously.

"Really! And since we're there, we might as well go around the corner to Bridger Way and pick up Malcolm Price at number 321." Claudia gave me a sideways glance. "Telephone 793–4199."

She and I know all kinds of important information about Blake and Malcolm, such as their addresses and phone numbers, what time they go to baseball practice, which is their favorite sugar-free gum, and which one likes chocolate milk and which one likes plain. So far we haven't had an opportunity to make use of any of it.

"Oh wow, Claudia! It *might* work. Parents love to carpool, and it sounds so reasonable."

We were walking very slowly, "dandering" as Mom calls it, because there's something else we know. We know the exact time the school bus arrives at school, and we know how to arrange it that we're right there when everyone gets off. Blake and Malcolm ride the bus.

It's hard to just stop and wait for it to come, so we listen for the motor in the distance and time our steps.

"You know what?" I said. "I think you'll have to ask Blake and Malcolm if they *want* to car-pool. I mean, we can't just arrange their lives for them. And you'd better ask them fast, before they make any other plans."

"Me? Why do *I* have to do it? Well, you have to come, too. . . ." Claudia stopped talking because we could hear the bus, and now we could see it, rattling and rolling around the corner the way it always does. I swear that bus must be a hundred years old.

We immediately put on our most nonchalant expressions and began to walk at a brisk pace, paying no attention at all to the bus as it shuddered and puffed to a stop. And there were Blake and Malcolm getting off. Blake was wearing stiff new jeans and a navy blue sweat shirt that said Yale on the chest.

I pushed Claudia forward so she was right in front of Malcolm on the sidewalk.

"Hi," she said to him, giving me a desperate backward look. "Er, Janey and I wondered if we could give you and Blake a ride to school?"

Malcolm pushed back his Dodger cap. "But we're *at* school," he said. "We took the bus."

"Oh." Claudia's mouth opened and closed. "OK," she said. "I forgot."

Then she cringed back toward me.

"We should have practiced," she said sadly.

23

j39451

5

As soon as we got into class, I remembered that it was my day to take care of Pebbles, who was already out of his cage and sniffing around everybody's feet. I pulled out his bottom tray, dumped the newspapers that were covered with his gross pebbles, and got a fresh paper from Mr. Puttinski's pile. Then I made sure Pebbles's water was clean, and I put today's alfalfa pellets and carrot tops into his bowl. Pebbles likes the tops of the carrots better than the rest. As usual, I watched Blake out of the corner of my eye.

Rosie Green was sitting at her desk, being quiet and reading. Pebbles had already undone the laces of both her tennis shoes and was busily nibbling on one of them. I think he goes mostly to Rosie because her feet are the biggest in the room, and they hold a fatal fascination for him. Before Rosie came, Pebbles used to go to Jefferson Ames, who is already five foot six and has feet to match. That little rabbit has a good measuring eye.

Rosie turned a page. Her face was all screwed up, and

she was leaning so close into the book that she didn't even notice what Pebbles was doing. Then she lifted him into her lap and sat stroking him. And she didn't even bother to retie her shoes.

Just after recess Putt-Putt asked if all eligible Rabbits had taken home the complete set of papers. All the Rabbits shouted yes.

The kids who weren't in the club and who hadn't bothered to read the books were whining and complaining now about how it was no fair and how *they* wanted to go to Rabbit night, too.

"Opportunity knocks but once, my friends," Putt-Putt said. "And this one's done knocked already."

Then he asked the eligible Rabbits if we'd talked it over with our parents and if there was anyone who couldn't or didn't want to go to the sleepover.

"Not want to go? Are you crazy, Mr. Puttinski?" Tina Semple asked. Tina is always shouting out to ask if someone or other is crazy. Claudia and I have decided that it's her subtle way of drawing attention to herself, since she's Sylvie Pedersen's best friend and Sylvie is so cute. Tina's got to get attention any way she can.

"OK. Is there anyone who may not be *able* to go?" Putt-Putt asked.

Claudia turned round and shook her head at me, but I put up my hand anyway. It's best to prepare ahead for possible disappointment.

"Janey?" Putt-Putt sounded shocked.

"I *may* not." I glanced sideways at Blake to see how he was taking my announcement. Unfortunately, he seemed to be taking it very well.

"That would be too bad, Janey. We'll hope for the best," Putt-Putt said.

Me, too, I thought.

Then he asked Sylvie Pedersen, who was supply monitor, to pass out the slips for WHO, WHAT, WHERE, WHEN, AND WHY. Sylvie was looking really yummy in a pinky red sweater and pinky red corduroys the color of strawberry slush. She had little silver barrettes in her hair, which is long and of course blond. Sylvie is always the first to find out about new trends. I'd never seen barrettes like these before. They almost looked like big paper clips. I bet Tina Semple will have some just like them tomorrow. Tina Semple is usually the second in trends, and the rest of us lag somewhere behind.

I noticed that when Sylvie gave Blake his paper, she said "Hi" to him and that he smiled. I'm almost sure she likes him.

WHO, WHAT, WHERE, WHEN, AND WHY is great. Putt-Putt says it helps teach us the components of a sentence. What we do is this. Each person writes a name on the top of the paper and folds it over. That's the WHO part. Usually we have somebody funny like Godzilla's grandmother or Dracula's sister, or else somebody cute like Michael Jackson or Brooke Shields or Pebbles. Then you pass the paper with the hidden name to the next desk for the WHAT. It could be FELL or JUMPED or WAS SHOVED. Then you fold the paper again and pass it on for the WHERE, and so on. When we finish with the WHY, the papers are unfolded, and you get to read out loud the one that has ended up on your desk. This can be embarrassing because sometimes there are really rude things on there. Putt-Putt doesn't allow us to use some words, which is just as well. But we always get one or two kids who put "fell in the toilet" or "got kicked in the butt," which makes me think there are some sixth-graders who don't have too much imagination.

At the end, when I opened mine to read it, I saw *Sylvie Pedersen* for the WHO.

I hate it when somebody does that.

Actually, nobody has ever started with Janey Winston, and I think that's probably not a very flattering sign. Sylvie's name comes up quite regularly.

"Sylvie Pedersen," I read, and everyone went, "Oh oh, Sylvie!" Sylvie smiled and took the paper clip out of her hair and put it back in the same place. I guess she's used to this.

"Sylvie Pedersen ate a mouse," I read.

"Oh, barf city!" Sylvie said, and Jefferson Ames pretended to throw up.

"OK, now. That's enough," Putt-Putt said. "We have the proper noun and the verb action. Go on, Janey."

Before I could go on, Jefferson Ames very rudely snatched the slip of paper right out of my hands. "Look!" he said. "It was Blake Conway who wrote Sylvie's name. That's *his* Day-Glo pen."

"You're nuts," Blake said, but I could see that the back of his neck had gone extremely red.

"Sit down, Jefferson," Putt-Putt said in his Mr. Puttinski voice.

Jefferson slid the paper onto Blake's desk beside his open workbook. "Check it out," Jefferson said. "Is that your Day-Glo pen or isn't it?"

I stole a quick glance at Sylvie, who was smiling her Mona Lisa smile, whatever that is.

Blake crumpled up the paper and stuffed it in his pocket.

"Lots of people have Day-Glo pens." Claudia turned and gave me a peppy look.

But it *was* Blake's pen. I knew it. Claudia's peppy look hadn't pepped me up a bit.

I'd always suspected Sylvie liked Blake. Now I was sus-pecting he liked her. And there they'd be, getting to know each other even *better* at the sleepover. Oh, if only I was brave enough to go! If only!

6

Our class has forty-five minutes for lunch, and I decided to rush to Mrs. Golden's room and see if Mom had called her yet and if I could find out anything.

"But I've already asked Rosie Green to eat with us," Claudia wailed. "What am I going to talk to her about? You should have warned me!"

"This is an emergency," I said, and Claudia sighed.

"I guess you're right. But hurry. I'll save you a place between me and Rosie. Good luck, Janey," she called after me.

I had two new book reports, which gave me a good reason anyway to go see Mrs. Golden.

Goldie's room is really little, with a sloping ceiling and no windows. It's up a set of back stairs, and it's not a classroom or even a real teacher's room because Goldie only works three days a week, and maybe they figure for three days she doesn't need a regular room. Goldie's a reading consultant who goes to other schools besides ours. She's truly wonderful, and she'd made her room wonderful, too. In fact, it's probably the best room in the whole school.

There are books everywhere, and book posters on the walls and ceiling. There are dinosaur models that dangle from hooks, and homemade kites, and a jungle of flower mobiles that you have to push through to get to her table. Stretching from wall to wall is Mrs. Golden's banner. It says: "It's not going to be magic if you don't practice." That's her motto, I guess, what she always says about reading and *why* she's all the time thinking up ways to get kids who aren't into it to start and keep going. Then somewhere along the line reading stops being a hassle and turns into the magic thing it really is.

Mrs. Golden was sitting at her long, cluttered-up table under her long fluorescent light, working on one of her projects. She always has a project. When I came in, she looked up, and we gave each other the Bunny Sign.

"Hi, Jane." She swiveled her chair around and tweaked a stick of celery from the green-banded bunch on the table. Goldie is always on a diet. She cradles a bundle of celery everywhere she goes, the way a movie star would cradle a bouquet of flowers. Except the movie star wouldn't keep pulling a flower from the bunch and eating it. Not unless she was pretty weird.

Mrs. Golden sometimes uses a stalk of celery to point to a book on a top shelf or a poster on the wall. I'm sure the person who invented celery never knew it was such useful stuff. She held the bunch toward me.

"Not right now," I said.

"Well, sit, honey."

I sat next to her.

"Did my mom call you yet?"

Mrs. Golden nodded and munched. "We had a nice chat. She says you're 'reading the world' now. I like that. It's very descriptive." Goldie nodded her head. "Reading the world, Jane." She pulled off another celery stick and chewed dreamily.

I put my two reports down beside her.

"Oh, thanks, hon. Do you need more books? I've got lots."

"I still have three," I said.

While she looked at my reports, I wondered how to ask her what else my mom had said besides that I was 'reading the world.' I needed to know about the crucial question and the even-more-crucial answer. But I didn't want to be rude and interrupt because Goldie has told us more than once that interrupting a person who is engrossed in reading is the most impolite thing you can do. So I sat and waited.

I love people whose names suit them so perfectly, and I've always hated mine. Plain Jane! One day I told Goldie that, and she took a book from a shelf and began to read me a love scene between Jane Eyre and Mr. Rochester.

" 'Oh, Jane! My hope—my love—my life' broke in anguish from his lips."

All at once the name Jane sounded like the most romantic and beautiful name on earth to me. Except that everyone calls me Janey, everybody except me and Mrs. Golden.

She gave me one of her golden smiles now. "I see you loved *Island of the Blue Dolphins.* Didn't you cry?"

I nodded, and she nodded, too, and began reading my second report.

I guess Mrs. Golden must have had an ordinary sort of name before she married Mr. Bertrand Golden, but that's hard to imagine. Everything about her is apropos, which means just right.

Her hair is golden. It couldn't really be that color, but it's terrific. She has golden skin, too. I'm not saying she doesn't wear some kind of gold-based makeup to help it along, but her real skin has to be a great color underneath to come out that good. All of Mrs. Golden is sort of buttery, and she wears funky clothes and lots of gold jewelry. I mean *lots*. There are some books I will associate for all my life with the musical accompaniment of Goldie's jangly bracelets as she read to us.

One time Jefferson Ames called her Mrs. T behind her back because of all the jewelry, which might have been a little bit funny, except that we'd *never* laugh at Mrs. Golden. Besides, she has hair, and Mr. T doesn't.

"Great book reports, Jane," she said, beaming at me and leaning across to pat my hand. Did I mention that she has two gold teeth on the side? I have never liked gold teeth, but on Goldie they just make her sparkle more.

"Let's record these on the chart," she said.

The chart is pinned on the slope of the wall. All the Rabbits' names are printed on the left-hand side, and then there are squares with red x's to show how many books each one of us has read. The book titles are squished in on the right-hand side.

Blake Conway's name is right above Claudia Fairfield's, and Malcolm Price's name is right above mine because it's in alphabetical order. Anyway, it's great because I can very subtly check out what Blake's been reading. His last title was *The Phantom Tollbooth*. I decided to read it myself next.

Then I noticed Rosie Green's name at the end of the list. She was the only person who had as many x's as I had. I looked at her list of books.

"Wow," I said. "Rosie Green's read a lot of good stuff. *A*

Tale of Two Cities, Travels with Charlie, The Caine Mutiny.
Hard, too."

Goldie found her red pen in the mess on her table. "Did you know Rosie's grandfather lives with her and her mother? He's going blind. I think Rosie reads to him a lot."

"Oh!" Thinking about Rosie reading to her going-blind grandfather made me feel really awful. She must be kind and nice, and all we'd done was tell her not to feed the rabbit lettuce. I pictured her sitting with him between four and midnight while her mom was at work. How sad!

Goldie added my two x's and stood back to admire them. "There, Jane. Good. Oh, by the way, when your mom called this morning . . ."

My heart began to thump really hard.

". . . she asked me if we'd be keeping the cafeteria lights on all night for the sleepover, and I told her 'no way.' We'd never get you guys to settle down till we turn them off. She said we'd better leave *some* on, though."

I tried to stand still and not pull on my hair, which is something I do if I'm nervous.

"Your mom said that when she went to boarding school, kids were always tripping over things in the dark. And she was telling me that Claudia Fairfield fell over a tree stump one night when she was up at Whispering Pines Camp and gave herself a nasty cut on her forehead. Of course she *should* have had her flashlight. That wasn't the camp's fault."

Goldie waved me invitingly toward the celery, but I shook my head.

"I told your mom we'll be leaving the bathroom lights on. They're right next to the cafeteria, and they'll shine in if we leave both doors open. She doesn't think that'll be enough, and you know what, Jane? She said she'll bring over a bunch of those little night lights, and we can plug them in all around." Goldie beamed. "Isn't that a smart idea? Then if you kids act up, I'll be able to pounce right away!" She bared her teeth and made claws with her golden nails. "I think it was really nice of your mother to be so concerned."

I didn't know I'd been holding my breath, but I guess I had because it suddenly exploded out of me.

"Well, good," I said. "Terrific. OK then." I was edging out. "Bye, Goldie . . . I mean, Mrs. Golden."

"Jane, wait a second. Take a look at the poetry tree before you go. It's turning out so well."

The tree was on the wall just inside the door, so I stopped. Immediately I saw Blake's poem. Mine was there, too, but I didn't bother to read it because I already knew what it said. Blake's was great. You have to use the letters of your first name for the first word in each line. Blake's poem had five lines for B-L-A-K-E.

Birds fly in the air
Lizards crawl everywhere
Ants run on the ground
Kangaroos leap around
Elephants have trunks and walk kerplunks.

"Kerplunks!" I said, without meaning to.

Goldie had come over beside me. She smiled. "You're reading Blake's. Isn't it terrific?"

"Terrific!" I said. Not as enthusiastically as I would normally because I was remembering something Goldie had said before we read Blake's poem. Something that might make it absolutely possible for me to go to the sleepover after all, something foolproof, so I wouldn't have to worry at all. I stood, dazed.

Goldie stepped back. "Do you like my dress, Jane? Bertrand bought it for me. When I put it on this morning, do you know what he said?" Her dress was a yellow tube with faint gray stripes from neckline to hem. Goldie cocked her head and smiled expectantly.

I tried to concentrate. "It is very unusual. What did Mr. Golden say?"

Goldie's wonderful smile widened. "He said I looked like an overripe banana. Needless to say, bananas are Bertrand's favorite fruit."

"I like them, too," I said.

And then this voice I knew was speaking behind me.

I swung around. It was Blake Conway! I was so flustered and trying to think of so many things at once that I forgot to give the Bunny Sign. He didn't either.

"I brought back the books and the reports, Mrs. Golden," he said. I noticed his dumb Day-Glo pen clipped to the pocket of his jeans.

"How come you're not going to the sleepover, Janey?" he asked. His face still had a bit of the strawberry color left around the ears.

"Oh . . . ah . . ." I couldn't believe he was asking me! Did he really want to know? And I never remembered his actually calling me by name before. I'd never been sure he really knew it.

"What do you mean not going?" Goldie asked, all alarmed.

"Oh, well, I think now maybe I *am* going."

Goldie smiled. "Oh sure. Now that your mom's talked to me."

"That's good then," Blake said. He thought it was good! Just wait till I told Claudia all this.

"So what have you got, Blake?" Goldie was taking his book reports, and I began edging away. Then I was skipping down the stairs saying kerplunks, kerplunks, kerplunks on every step and feeling so good I could hardly stand it.

7

On Tuesday night, Dad and I decided to make a trial run at school. We unplugged the little night lights from our house and took them with us.

"Let's see just how dark it is going to be at your sleepover," Dad said.

He'd called ahead already, and Hero, the school custodian, met us on the front steps and unlocked the doors. Of course, now that I had the plan, I wouldn't really need the night lights. But a little backup never hurt.

I couldn't believe how creepy Fred Barrington Elementary was at night. Our feet clattered in the silence as we went along the hallway to the cafeteria. I stayed safe between Hero and Dad, away from the dark open doors of the classrooms on either side, and I tried not to breathe in the smells of floor polish and bathroom disinfectant.

"How's Macho Rabbit?" I asked Hero, just for something ordinary to say. Macho belongs to Hero, who likes Pebbles so much that he got himself a rabbit to keep at home. One day he brought Macho in to meet Pebbles, and they got along really well.

"Macho's great," Hero said. "My girlfriend takes him to work with her every day so he won't be lonely. She's a hairdresser, and she says all her ladies love to hold him."

"Lucky Macho," I said. I thought about Pebbles upstairs in his box, and I hoped he wasn't too lonely or too afraid of the dark. In school, at night, there sure is a lot of dark around.

When we got to the cafeteria, we discovered there were only four electrical outlets. Behind the serving counter, in the kitchen area, there were more. Dad plugged in all the night lights. Then Hero opened the bathroom doors, the way they'd be on Friday night, and turned off the big overhead fluorescents. Man! What a dark pit! Those little night lights were totally swallowed by the blackness. Things started crawling in the bottom of my throat.

"The plan," I told myself, and I tried to hold onto that. But I needed to hold onto Dad, too, and I grabbed for his hand.

When I was little and in the closet, I thought the vacuum was a bad fairy with a hump on her back, or sometimes a man with a sack, come to carry me away. Those dark hulking refrigerators that gleamed in the kitchen were almost as bad. I shivered. "You won't even see them," I told myself. "You won't be here when it's dark.

"Looks OK, huh?" Hero ruffled my hair. "You wouldn't need any more light than that unless you were a sunflower."

I nodded, trying to smile. All I wanted was to get out of here right now, back to the warm, bright safety of home. Did I really want to go through with this? Even for the games? And those quiet, friendly reading times while we were tucked in our sleeping bags? Even though Blake would be there? Did I?

Dad kept the inside light on in the car as we drove home, which is something he doesn't usually do.

"Would you like *me* to volunteer to stay over Friday night?" he asked, glancing at me sideways. "Goldie and Mr. Puttinski would probably be glad of an extra person."

"I don't think so. But thanks, Dad." Wow! How awful! Imagine going to the sleepover and being *the only person there with a parent!* I debated letting Dad in on the plan, so he'd know it might not be too bad. But there are some things a parent will never go for, and I suspected this plan would be one of them. "I'll be fine," I said.

Claudia called as soon as we got home.

She was quiet for a minute when I told her that even with the night lights, the cafeteria was still pretty dark. "Want to join zippers in our sleeping bags and make a double?" she asked.

Nice Claudia!

"Nah, it'll be OK," I said. I thought about telling her, too, about the plan, but even with Claudia I'm ashamed of being such a big baby. So I changed the subject instead. "All we have to do now is get Blake and Malcolm to ride with us," I said. "And tomorrow's the day to ask them."

"Tomorrow?" Claudia said faintly. "Tomorrow?"

The next morning we asked Rosie if she wanted to come with us and help invite them.

"Why?" She looked taken aback. "I thought it would be just *us.*"

We gave her our convincing story about how car pools save gas and parents, and how Claudia's brother had offered to drive Friday night so he could have the car after, and how he wouldn't mind *who* we picked up and took to the sleepover.

"And if you like, my mom could come get us Saturday morning, Rosie," I said. "I mean, with your mother working late, and your grandfather and all." My words stuttered to a stop because of the new, nervous look on Rosie's face.

"How do *you* know about my grandfather?" she asked.

"Well, Goldie told me . . ." I could swear Rosie got white as paper, as if we'd discovered her most awful secret. That was really dumb, because knowing that she read to her grandfather and probably looked after him when her mom was at work made me think she must be extra nice.

She stared down at her feet. I have to admit, if you looked down at all, her feet *would* be hard to miss since her tennis shoes were bright pink and big as bathtubs. "It's OK," she said at last. "My mom will drive. She's always up before nine on Saturdays." She smiled at me. "I'm glad you're coming, Jane."

I smiled, too. "Thanks. So do you want to come with us at recess and ask the boys?"

"Uh-uh." Rosie backed away. "You can just tell me what they say."

So Claudia and I were on our own, which to be honest, was probably better.

I was dreading it, though. We'd have to be real casual, cool, and nonchalant. But at recess we didn't have a chance to ask them casually, coolly, and nonchalantly because Putt-Putt had organized a game of Hit Pin Fist Ball.

I'm not sure, but I think maybe Putt-Putt invented Hit Pin Fist Ball. There are two teams. One fields, the other bats, though there is no bat and you hit the pitcher's ball with your fist. Orange-colored cones mark the bases, and you get a point for every cone that's still standing as you run past it on the way home. Of course, the fielders are trying to knock the cone down before you get to it. Blake and I are on the same team, and when I got a good hit, I could hear him yelling, "Run, Janey, run!"

Crumbs! He still *remembered* my name. I ran with all my might.

When I got to home base, all four cones were still up.

"OK!" Blake said.

And then Jefferson Ames yelled, "Did anybody ever tell you you run just like a duck, Janey?" He turned his feet out and flapped his arms.

I thought I was going to die.

"So what if she does?" Blake said. "She made us four points."

Just then the bell rang for the end of recess, and we all rushed to line up at the water fountain.

"What did Blake mean when he said, 'What if she does?' " I asked Claudia. "Does that mean he thinks I run like a duck, too?"

"He was sticking up for you, that's all," Claudia said.

But I wasn't so sure.

I watched Malcolm and him pushing and shoving at the front of the line. "We could ask them about the car pool now," I whispered to Claudia. "Perfect chance."

"No way," Claudia said. "We need to get them by themselves. What if they say no in front of everyone? It would be too embarrassing."

Then I had a great idea. "Maybe we should call them?"

Claudia's eyes opened wide. "Oh, man! Do we dare?"

"They'd at least be alone." The thought of calling them was making my breathing funny.

"And if they sound too horrified, we could pretend it's not us," Claudia said. "Oh, let's."

It's really OK to call a boy. Probably girls like Sylvie

Pedersen do it all the time. Actually, girls like Sylvie Pedersen probably don't have to. But telling yourself it's OK and believing it are two different things.

We'd decided to phone from Claudia's house to escape Oriana and Rachel, and it was ten after three when we got there. Shauna, who sits for my little sisters till I get home, likes to leave at three-thirty, so we didn't have time for much pondering.

Upstairs, in his studio, Claudia's dad coughed his dry, barky cough. We'd yelled up to him that we were here, and he'd answered, but he'd probably forgotten us already. Mr. Fairfield is the most totally absorbed person I've ever seen. That's what Claudia's mother says about him, and she's right. Claudia's mother says a burglar could come in while Mr. Fairfield's painting and rip off the whole house and Mr. Fairfield would never notice—not unless the guy tried to take his easel or his paints or canvas. So Claudia and I can feel really private down here in the living room.

"Who's going to do it?" Claudia asked.

"You," I said. "*You* call Blake. *I'll* call Malcolm. That way they won't know. It will confuse them if they already guess we like them."

Claudia thought this over. "That's smart, Janey, but it seems like a waste. I mean, I don't particularly want to talk to Blake, and I may never in my whole life have such a perfect excuse to call Malcolm."

"It would also be easier to take rejection from a person who isn't important to you," I pointed out.

Claudia nodded. "That's true."

We flipped to see who'd go first and I won, which meant Claudia had to dial. I called the number out loud for her, and inside me my heart was suddenly going "kerplunk, kerplunk, kerplunk," heavy as an elephant's feet.

"Suppose . . ." Claudia began and then she said, "Sh!"

though I wasn't the one talking, and said into the phone, "May I please speak to Blake?" She covered the mouthpiece and told me, "She's gone to get him.".

"Who's she?"

"His mother."

"Maybe it was his sister. He has a sister who's fifteen."

"I know. But this was for sure his mother."

"What does she sound like?"

"Normal. Just like a mother. When Blake comes, I'm going to say . . ." She shushed me again. "Blake? Hi! This is Claudia. You know, Claudia Fairfield?"

I leaned weakly against the wall. Man, was I ever glad I wasn't the one doing the talking. I'd have fainted by now.

"We were wondering . . . my friend Janey and I . . . you know, Janey Winston?"

"Claudia!" I moaned.

"We were wondering if . . . you see my brother's driving us to the sleepover on Friday night and Rosie Green's mother . . ." She stopped again, and I could see that she was listening. Watching her listening and not knowing what she was listening to was driving me bats. It's truly awful only being able to hear one side of a conversation. Especially an important conversation like this one.

"Oh, well. I didn't know," Claudia was saying, and I was tugging her arm and going, "What? What?"

There was more listening while I died, and Claudia held up her hand for me to die more quietly. "Well, sure. Great," she said at last. Then, "OK. See you tomorrow probably," and she hung up the phone.

"What? What?" I begged again.

"He knew already about the car-pooling. Rosie Green's mother was going to work, and she saw Blake's mother in their garden, and they made the arrangements. Blake's mother has decided *she'll* drive Friday night."

"Maybe she doesn't trust your brother." I was totally overcome by these new developments.

"I don't blame her," Claudia said. "So they'll be picking us up. And they'll be picking up Malcolm." It wasn't hard for me to see that at the thought of Malcolm, Claudia was totally overcome, too.

"*And* Rosie," I said. "None of this would have happened if it hadn't been for Rosie." I was feeling guilty all over again about Rosie and trying to make up.

I leaned against the wall again, imagining Blake's mother driving up to our house, and maybe Blake running up our steps, ringing our doorbell. Crumbs! And I might get to sit next to him in the car, and after, in the cafeteria, we might talk and get to be friends.

I was thinking about the cafeteria, all lit up and decorated the way it had been for the Valentine's party, and suddenly everything changed and I saw it with the shadows slithering down from the ceiling, the ghost glimmer of the night lights.

No. I wouldn't let myself think about that part of it. I wouldn't. Besides, it would only be for a little while. Then I'd be safe.

8

All day Thursday kids were reading. They were reading as they walked along the halls, in the bathrooms, or secretly, when they were supposed to be working in their workbooks.

Malcolm Price had a bookmark that said, *"Buzz off I'm reading,"* and he held it in front of his face when Putt-Putt announced decimal division time. But Putt-Putt wasn't having any of that.

Claudia and I had thanked Rosie for having her mom make the arrangements for tomorrow night, but Rosie had just shrugged as if all this wonderful, exciting stuff about to happen wasn't even important.

Before recess Blake gave Claudia a note. I watched her open it, look at Blake, and nod. It was probably about picking us up tomorrow night, but still I felt really jealous, and I wished he'd given it to me. Maybe I was too clever, having Claudia call him. Now she's the one getting notes from him.

She passed it back to me.

"My mom will pick you and Janey up at ten to six," Blake had written in his hateful Day-Glo pen.

I slid the note carefully between the pages of my reader. My first letter, ever, from him. If I squinted and left out a couple of words, he could almost be writing to me about a date.

"What's up with Pebbles?" Jefferson Ames asked. "He's acting weird."

Putt-Putt looked down at Pebbles, who was huddled close to Tina Semple's leg. "What's weird about him?"

"He's not doing it now. He *was* biting at himself. Maybe he's got cooties."

"Are you crazy?" Tina shrieked. "Rabbits don't have cooties." But she pulled her legs quickly to the other side of the desk.

Rosie Green ran up and lifted Pebbles into her lap.

"He could have gotten another electric shock," Malcolm said, which was possible as Pebbles had once chewed all the way through the computer wire. A couple of the boys went to check, but the wire just had a few rabbit teeth marks, nothing special.

"He's *shivering*," Rosie said.

"I certainly hope he's not getting rabbit flu." Sylvie leaned as far away from Rosie as possible. "He might be contagious. You should put him down."

"I bet he has nits stuck in his fur," Jefferson Ames said. "Have a look for them, Rosie. They're probably jumping off him this very minute, and now they're stuck all over you."

Pebbles leaped off Rosie's knees and headed for his box.

"You hurt his feelings," Rosie said and ran to get him

again, but Putt-Putt told her to leave Pebbles alone and go on with her work.

When Claudia and I went into the bathroom at lunchtime, we were just in time to hear Sylvie Pedersen describing the new pj's she'd bought for the sleepover.

She and Tina Semple were hair-brushing in front of the mirror. A bunch of non-Rabbits were hanging around, listening and looking jealous.

"I think they're going to be perfect for the sleepover," Sylvie was saying. "They're fuzzy pink, sort of plush . . . you know the kind, Tina?"

Tina nodded. "How darling!"

"And they have feet attached on," Sylvie said. "Can you imagine? Like little kids' pj's, but really adorable."

Claudia and I pushed toward the mirror so we could fix our hair. Claudia only finger-combs hers, there's so little of it. I fished in my purse for my brush. In the mirror I could see Tina admiring Sylvie, who was shaking her hair out and brushing it from underneath. I could almost hear it crackle.

"And here's the all-time cutest thing," Sylvie said. "At the back there's this darling little puff of a tail, like a bunny's!"

"Won't it be hard to sleep on?" Tina asked.

We all waited in suspense.

"Uh-uh. It's *soft*. Just like a ball of fluff."

Claudia gave me the raised eyebrow look in the mirror. Usually I can interpret Claudia's looks, but I wasn't sure about this one. I went back to watching Sylvie. She really is pretty, and it was *her* name that Blake had written with his Day-Glo pen. When she shook back her hair, it rippled like pale yellow silk. Actually, I don't mind my own hair, which is the color of the leaves on the copper birch that we tagged on our Arbor Day walk. Sometimes Mom calls it

"Irish setter red" and tells me how lucky I am to be so un-ordinary. But when I stand next to Sylvie like this, I don't feel un-ordinary at all.

"Didn't your little sister have pj's with feet?" Claudia asked me suddenly, leaning close to the mirror to check her pale pink Chapstick, which is the only lipstick she and I are allowed to wear. "Didn't Oriana's have a little trap-door at the back so your mom could change her diaper?" She leaned away from the mirror and began finger-comb-ing her hair again. "And even when Oriana was out of diapers, didn't your mom keep getting her that kind so she could use the bathroom without taking everything off? Do yours have a trapdoor in back, Sylvie?"

"Are you crazy, Claudia Fairfield?" Tina asked coldly. "Of *course* Sylvie's don't."

I tried not to laugh. A trapdoor on Sylvie's behind!

"What time are Malcolm and Blake picking us up to-morrow night?" Claudia asked me, real casually, but also real loudly.

It was astonishing how quiet the bathroom became, as if someone had turned off the noise switch.

"Six o'clock," I said, just as casually. "No, I think Blake said ten to six."

Claudia frowned a fake frown. "Are you sure? What ex-actly did he say in his note?"

Wow! Did we have the attention of every single girl in the bathroom now! Sylvie even had a small worry wrinkle between her perfect eyebrows. "How come they're picking you up?" she asked. "You hardly even know them."

"I bet you *asked* them," Tina Semple said loudly. Tina is no fool.

"As a matter of fact, we didn't," Claudia said. "Come on, Janey."

We were pretty pleased with ourselves as we swaggered

out and headed back to class. "Wasn't that perfect?" Claudia asked. "That was the best time I've had in that bathroom since I started school."

"Pink fuzzy pj's with a darling tail in back," I said thoughtfully. "Sylvie's going to be pretty cute all right. What do you bet Tina Semple gets some just like them before tomorrow night?"

"Do you suppose *everyone* will be wearing pj's after all?" Claudia asked.

She and I had planned on sleeping in corduroys and sweat shirts and white socks, and we'd told Rosie to wear the same.

"I don't *have* any real nice pj's," I said. "Mostly I have nightgowns."

"I'd like funny ones," Claudia said. "Red long johns. Or those convict kind with your prisoner number on the front."

We lingered outside the door of room nine.

"We *could* walk to the mall right after school," Claudia said. "You could call your mom, and she could ask Shauna to stay a bit extra. And I'd call Dad, and then we could dash home, and you have that $18 left from Christmas and I have $12. . . ."

Putt-Putt was standing in the doorway. "Spelling test, ladies," he said cheerfully. "Shopping plans must be postponed." I swear, there are times when I think Putt-Putt loves to be the bearer of bad news.

"Want to do it, Janey?" Claudia whispered, and I nodded. "But we have to ask Rosie, too."

At afternoon recess we asked Rosie if she wanted to come with us, but she said that she had to go to the main library after school. I decided it was probably to get more books to read to her grandfather and we shouldn't try to get her to change her mind. Actually and honestly, of course, I didn't want her to change her mind.

Claudia and I rushed home after school, and everything was OK, and then we headed straight for the mall.

"Didn't you think Rosie acted funny yesterday when she talked about her grandfather?" I asked Claudia.

"What do you mean, funny?"

"Nervous. Kind of scared because we'd found out about him."

"About her grandfather?" Claudia pondered this for a few steps. "Maybe he's not *really* her grandfather. Maybe she kidnapped him, and she's keeping him prisoner."

"Oh sure," I said. As I've mentioned before, Claudia can sometimes get carried away.

We headed straight for Buffums because we know they have a good girls' underwear department. We pretty much know who has the best departments in each store.

Usually, when you want something real super, you can't find it, but Buffums is very dependable. Claudia found cute bright blue pj's made like a baseball uniform. On the front it said, SWEET DREAMS, DODGERS, which was very apropos. The Dodgers had hoped to win the pennant this year, and they didn't even get to first base. That's my father's baseball joke. And since Malcolm Price always wears his Dodger cap, Claudia's Dodger uniform made them almost a matched pair.

I got pale pink pj's striped with white, like peppermint candy. A frill of lace came down the front beside the buttons, and for an extra four dollars I got matching pink and white ballet slippers. "You're sure I don't look too babyish?" I asked Claudia.

"Uh-uh, no way!"

"I don't look like a duck?"

"I've never heard of a pink-and-white striped duck in ballet slippers," Claudia said. "Unless it's some foreign job."

"It's just that I'm nervous right now of anything ducky,"

49

I explained. "And you don't think Sylvie will think I copied her, getting pink? Slippers are almost like having built-in feet. . . ."

"You are driving me nuts," Claudia said.

We felt pretty good, especially since we each had enough money left to have a double-dip chocolate-chip ice-cream cone to eat on the way home from the mall.

The clock on top of the Security Bank said ten minutes past four. I gobbled down the last bite of my cone. "We have to hurry," I said. "Mom promised Shauna I'd be back by four-thirty." Being with Claudia, buying the pajamas, talking and everything had made me put the terrible blackness that waited for me out of my thoughts—at least out of the thoughts that filled the front of my head. Somewhere, way back, the fear waited to jump. It waited to get me alone, later. *Remember, I have the plan,* I told it. *I'm ready for you.*

Claudia nudged me, licked her fingers clean, and made the Bunny Sign over her head. "Look, there's Rosie."

It was Rosie, coming down the steps of the main library. When she saw us, she set down the big white book bag she was carrying and signed back. The bag said KCET on the side, and it was so heavy it was ready to topple over. Rosie stood in front of it, waiting for us. And why was I getting this nervous feeling again? Rosie bent down, made sure the bag wouldn't fall, stood on one foot, then the other, smiled, frowned, bit at her nails.

"We just got the cutest pj's," Claudia said "Mine are blue and Janey's are pink."

"That's good." Rosie didn't seem immensely interested.

"We told you we'd decided on pj's, didn't we?" I asked.

Rosie nodded.

"Was Pebbles OK when you left?" I asked, thinking Pebbles's health might be what was worrying her.

"I guess so. Putt-Putt says he probably just needs to be left alone. Putt-Putt says any rabbit in a sixth-grade class must sometimes crave a little solitude."

Claudia grinned. "That sounds like Putt-Putt."

Rosie had moved a little, and I couldn't help seeing her books, which were sticking out of the top of the bag. *The Day of the Jackal,* which is a real adult novel, *How Green Was My Valley,* and then I saw *Frog and Toad Together,* which is a total baby book and one of Rachel's favorites. She and Oriana always ask for it when I read to them at night. I guess Rosie noticed the way my head was tilted, checking out the titles, and she moved again to hide the bag—but not before I'd spotted the corner of a Dr. Seuss book, *One Fish Two Fish Red Fish Blue Fish,* which is a *real* baby book.

"Well," Rosie said. "I've got to go."

"We do, too. See you tomorrow in school."

We hurried on. Once I looked back, and Rosie was walking the other way, the heavy book bag pulling her over on one side.

"I don't understand this," I said. "Did you see the books she had? Hard ones, easy ones . . . I mean, what a crazy mixture!"

"Maybe she likes to read crazy mixtures. *I* like picture books, too. I *love Babar.*"

"*One Fish Two Fish Red Fish Blue Fish?*" I asked.

"Well, maybe she kidnapped a kid sister for herself, too, and she reads to her *and* to her grandfather," Claudia said.

Sometimes Claudia definitely does get carried away.

9

It was ten of six Friday night, and I was *ready*.

Dad had stopped by school on his way home and plugged in the night lights. "You going to be OK with them, honey-bun?" he whispered to me.

"I think so." My voice didn't sound so sure, but that wasn't only because of the night lights. Now that it was almost time, my clever plan didn't seem as possible as it had a couple of days back.

I'd checked my flashlight and brought extra batteries, though a flashlight isn't much good to chase away the dark. All it does is scatter the light in one narrow passageway, making the blackness blacker on either side.

I'd checked out my books for the sleepover: *The Phantom Tollbooth,* which I'd managed to find on Goldie's rack today, and *The Best Christmas Pageant Ever.* Claudia had read it, and she said it made her fall down laughing. I thought funny might help tonight when the dark began to creep around the edges of the cafeteria. I just hoped *The Phantom Tollbooth* wasn't scary.

I buckled my backpack. "I *think* I'm ready," I said, fluttering around the living room, peering out the window, sitting down, standing up. Fortunately, Oriana and Rachel were in their room playing with my old Barbie doll, plus all her clothes that I'd given them right after dinner. I would have given them anything to keep them upstairs and out of the way.

When the doorbell rang, I almost jumped out of my body, but it was only Claudia and her mother, carrying Claudia's stuff between them.

"How's Mr. Fairfield's new painting going?" Dad asked. He's always interested in Mr. Fairfield's paintings because he can't understand why anybody buys them and pays so much money for them. Dad says even Oriana could draw a better goat in the middle of a blank field than Mr. Fairfield draws.

Mrs. Fairfield sighed. "It's coming along." Mrs. Fairfield sighs quite a lot over both Mr. Fairfield and his paintings. Claudia says it's because she doesn't like his being so absorbed.

Claudia and I stood close. "Are you nervous?" she asked me.

I nodded.

"Me, too. Feel my hands!" They were like two dead frogs.

She made her voice even lower. "Are you *really* OK?" This time I knew she was talking about my problem.

"I think so," I mumbled back.

"We'll hold hands after lights out if you like. Mine will have warmed up by then, and no one will see."

Claudia is really a good, true friend.

"I was thinking," she whispered. "Probably when they

come, the boys will be in the front of the car beside Blake's mom. And the three of us will sit in back. I just wish *my* mom would go home. I don't want her walking out to the car with us. You know how she is." Claudia rolled her eyes. I knew. Mrs. Fairfield might say something awful that she thought was funny. Such as, "Remember, boys! Kissing is off limits. No hand-holding either unless you ask permission first." Horrors!

"I've *warned* her," Claudia said.

And then the doorbell rang again, and though I'd been semi-listening for it, this time I really jumped out of my body. I could see it, standing there, in living color, like a wax dummy with no Janey inside.

Claudia gave me a little nudge. *"You* go."

"My legs . . ." I began. These heavy block legs wouldn't move me as far as the door.

"We'll both . . ." Claudia began, and then Oriana and Rachel came rocketing down the stairs and flung themselves past us. They fought over the handle, got the door open, and there was Blake. Blake in person, wearing his stiff turned-up jeans and a sweat shirt with READ BOOKS printed across the chest. Very apropos. Even though I'd imagined it a hundred times, it was hard for me to believe it was really him, standing at *my* door.

He peered past Oriana and Rachel, probably boggled by the crowd in our living room and by my two little sisters tugging at his hands. And now, Jock had unearthed himself from his flowerpot. Jock "unearthing" is another of Dad's jokes. The dumb cat was purring like a lawnmower and rubbing himself against Blake's legs.

"I'm Blake. Blake Conway."

Oriana gazed up admiringly. "I'm Oriana. Janey got new pajamas. They're pink and white."

"Oh. Good." Blake looked a little taken aback. I wished I

could have killed Oriana right there and then and been rid of her forever. I gave Mom a tight-lipped, meaningful look.

"All right, you little girls. Back upstairs," she said, too late, of course.

"Let's get your things out," Dad said to us, smoothly interrupting, not soon enough either. He lifted our two sleeping bags.

We were like a procession heading for Mrs. Conway's station wagon. "How embarrassing!" Claudia whispered. "Now, if my mom says something, we can just give up and stay home."

I was too embarrassed myself to even answer. "Janey has new pajamas." A good thing I didn't get new underpants, or Oriana would have told him that, too!

We marched down the path. First Blake, then my dad, then me, then Claudia, then Claudia's mom, then my mom, then Oriana and Rachel, who, of course, were not about to miss anything, then Jock, who must have felt the same way. A parade, for Pete's sake!

Blake's mother was standing at the back of a blue station wagon with the hatch open.

"Hi," she said. "I'm Carrie Conway."

The grownups all shook hands and said nice things to each other. Blake had disappeared inside the station wagon. I studied Mrs. Conway secretly. She didn't look a bit like Blake, and her hair was longer and straighter and blacker than most mothers' hair. She had a red scarf tied around it and knotted at the back.

Dad and the rest of us stowed our stuff away.

"Have a good time," Mom said and hugged me.

Then Dad hugged me. Then the two little girls hugged me. I almost expected Jock to put up his paws.

Rachel produced something from behind her back and

said, "Oriana and I bought you this." It was a small square package, wrapped the way Rachel wraps, all bunchy and lopsided. "Smell," she said, standing on tiptoe and sticking the package under my nose. "It's soap. So you can wash and smell nice. It cost 89 cents, and it's called 'Wild Flowers.' Oriana wanted to get you 'Mint' because the box was prettier, but you wouldn't want to smell like *mint*."

"Not really," I said. "And someone might try to make jelly out of me." I sniffed the bar again to please them and gave them each another hug. I guess, if you absolutely have to have little sisters, these two are about the best you could expect.

I was relieved when Mrs. Fairfield didn't say anything to me and Claudia except, "Be good." And I could tell by the way Claudia let out her breath that she was relieved, too. With Mrs. Fairfield, you never know.

Everybody looked solemn as if we were blasting off to Mars or somewhere. Of course, I knew my mom and dad were worried about me and trying not to show it.

"OK, climb aboard," Mrs. Conway said cheerfully. "One in front and one in back with the boys."

Oh no! Claudia and I dug each other with our elbows and hung back. This was an unexpected development. We were going to be separated. And now, with the hatch closed, we could plainly see that Rosie was in front beside the driver and the two guys were in back.

I tried to push Claudia ahead, and she tried to push me. *I* didn't want to be all by myself and next to the boys. I mean, when you're imagining stuff, that seems wonderful. But in real life, what it is is embarrassing. I wanted to sit safely next to Rosie. So did Claudia.

"Oh help," Claudia muttered, and then I realized that she'd managed to slip around me and was climbing in front.

The motor was beginning to get that loud, impatient sound, and Mrs. Fairfield looked naughty, as if she'd just thought up a clever parting remark.

I quickly got in beside Blake and closed the door.

"Hi." Malcolm gave me the Bunny Sign. "Fine night for a sleepover."

"Yes, really." I moved a little so there'd be more space between me and Blake.

Rosie turned and said, "Hi, Jane."

"Hi, Rosie."

We were bumping down our street now. Mrs. Conway's car seemed to be the bumpy kind.

"How come she calls you Jane instead of Janey?" Blake asked.

"I don't know," I said.

"I don't know either," Rosie said.

There hadn't been room for my book bag in the trunk, and I squeezed it between me and Blake. *The Phantom Tollbooth* was rather visible on top. When we stopped for the light on the corner of Hudson, Blake said, "Oh, *The Phantom Tollbooth*. I just read that. It's terrific, isn't it?"

"I haven't started it yet."

"You'll really like it."

"I like fantasy stuff," I said.

"Me, too. Did you read *A Wrinkle in Time?*"

"Yes. It was great." I couldn't believe this. I was having a long, interesting, super-intelligent conversation with Blake Conway. Truly, books are magic all right—and not only for reading.

"What is that smell?" Malcolm asked, sniffing hard.

"My soap." I shoved it farther down in the bag.

Blake sniffed, too. "It's nice."

Sometimes I absolutely love my little sisters.

"I have *The Dune Story Book* for tonight," Blake said.

"Goldie told me it's good, too. Do you want me to keep it for you after?"

"That would be wonderful."

"I like riddle books myself," Malcolm announced. "What do you get when you cross a rabbit with a beetle?"

Claudia half turned. "What?" she asked.

"Bugs Bunny," Malcolm said, and we all laughed.

"And speaking of rabbits, is Pebbles OK?" Mrs. Conway asked.

"Yes," Rosie said. "I helped Mr. Puttinski carry his box to the cafeteria today. He's kind of mopey."

"Putt-Putt?" Malcolm asked.

"No, Pebbles."

"I'm sure he'll be OK," Blake's mom said. "Well, here we are."

We were bumping to a stop in front of school. The night of the sleepover had really arrived. And I was kerplunking again.

10

Goldie was waiting on the school steps. The streetlights made an angel's halo around her hair and polished the bald head of the man with her. She gave the Bunny Sign as we began to pile out.

"Claudia, Rosie, Jane, Blake, Malcolm, may I present my husband, Bertrand Golden," she said. "He didn't want to stay home!"

We all said "Hi," and then Blake's mother came out and was introduced, and we began lugging our stuff up the steps.

"Bye," Blake's mom said. "Have a good time. Don't keep Mrs. Green waiting in the morning."

Then we were all trooping down the lighted hallways.

It didn't seem scary at all now, with everybody talking and with Malcolm and Blake right in front of us. Malcolm even had his Dodger cap turned backward for the occasion, which I thought looked pretty zippy. But Claudia whispered that she liked it better on him the other way.

Tina Semple came running toward us, chased by Jefferson Ames. Running in the hallway! It was like running in church! And no one was stopping them . . . no teacher, no hall monitor, no cranky Mrs. Lorenzo from the office. What freedom!

"Leave me alone, Jefferson Ames." Tina was laughing as she darted into the third-grade classroom with Jefferson after her. He had a cootie catcher over his thumb and finger, the kind you make by folding a square of paper, and he kept snapping it in the air behind Tina and yelling, "Cootie catcher. Cootie catcher."

Rosie gave an exasperated sigh. "He's still pretending Tina got cooties from Pebbles. And Pebbles is the cleanest little rabbit in the world!"

"Nobody pays any attention to Jefferson Ames," I said, hoping this was true and that nobody had paid any attention when he said I ran like a duck. I have noticed that I've become very aware of my feet, though, so I guess *I* paid attention.

"Jefferson! Tina!" Mrs. Golden called. "You're perfectly at liberty to run in the hallway, but let's stay out of the classrooms, please."

My gosh, school sure was different at night!

Tina shot out of the other door with Jefferson behind her. She was all pink, and I could tell she liked being chased by a boy, even if it was only Jefferson Ames with a cootie catcher.

The empty school bounced with light and noises that seemed to be coming from everywhere. Already I was loving it and wishing this part could go on and on and that night would never come. But of course it always does.

"Can there really only be twelve Rabbits, Goldie?" Mr.

Golden asked and raised his bushy eyebrows, which for some reason looked very apropos with his bald head.

The tables in the cafeteria had been pushed back, and music drifted softly from Mr. Puttinski's stereo on the kitchen counter. He stopped sifting through a pile of records to wave to us. The kids who were here already had spread their sleeping bags on the floor and piled their stuff beside them. A big bunch of balloons was tied to the back of one of the chairs, their strings so long that the balloons swayed close to the ceiling. Pebbles stood on his back legs chewing on the tyings.

"He looks OK, Rosie," I said, and Rosie nodded. Actually it's not real easy to see *how* a rabbit's looking, health-wise, under all that fur. But he was doing his usual chewing, which must be a good sign.

Sylvie Pedersen sat like a princess on her pale blue sleeping bag, brushing her hair. I guessed the bag beside hers was Tina's. "Hi, everybody," she called, waving her brush and giving the Bunny Sign. "There's lots of room over here." Maybe she was waving to everybody, but she was looking and smiling directly at Blake. Honestly, she has such nerve. But the one who went straight across and dumped her stuff next to Sylvie was Rosie Green. Sylvie opened her mouth and closed it again. There wasn't much she could say. A bunny is a friend to every other bunny—Rabbit Rule Number 6.

"Where do *you* want to be, Janey?" Claudia asked.

I could see that there was a boys' side and a girls' side in the cafeteria, just the way there always is at parties.

"Let's go next to Rosie," I said, which was perfect because I knew that when the bathroom doors were opened later, the path of light would fall right there, and I'd be safe till I put my plan into action.

So that's where we went, with me next to Rosie and Claudia on my other side.

And then, wonder of wonders, I realized Blake was standing beside me, digging around in his backpack.

Claudia and I had time to exchange one meaningful look while his head was bent. I also had time for a quick peek at Sylvie Pedersen's astonished face before Blake glanced up.

He'd taken a book from his backpack. "This is the one I was telling you about, Janey. I bought it, so if you want, you can borrow it after."

"Oh thanks." I was overcome again by the power and influence and helpfulness of books. This one was a paperback, *The Dune Story Book.* Under the title, and above the picture of two guys in spacesuits, it said "Can Paul uncover the secrets of the desert planet and save the galaxy from the evil emperor?"

"Neat," I said. "I bet he can."

Blake pulled out another book. "I brought this one, too. I'm a pretty fast reader."

It was called *The Castle of Llyr,* and the picture showed a giant cat, a million times bigger than Jock. "Princess Eilonwy is about to be captured," I read, and looked up at Blake. "I hope they don't plan on feeding her to this monster cat."

Blake grinned. "Really!" Blake has quite a large gap between his two front teeth, which Claudia says he ought to have fixed, but which I think is very attractive.

"Who's talking about *cats*?" Sylvie asked loudly, uncurling herself from her sleeping bag. "*I've* brought two Garfield books. I've got the brand-new one, Blake, if you'd like to borrow it."

"Sure. Thanks." Blake didn't sound all that interested.

But I reminded myself that because he wasn't interested in Garfield did not mean he was not interested in Sylvie.

"Who's still missing?" Mr. Puttinski called, and just then Chip and Betty Wu, who are twins, came in lugging their stuff.

"Great!" Putt-Putt said. "All present and correct. Let's get this sleepover on the road."

We stood around him while he went over again the way it was going to be. On the stereo was some kind of music that sounded like wind blowing and waves crashing against rocks.

"Six-thirty till seven, reading," Putt-Putt said. "Seven to seven-thirty, Quiet Ball."

Malcolm rolled his eyes. "Oh oh, Jefferson, you might as well not bother." We all laughed because Jefferson is rotten at Quiet Ball. Once you speak you're out of the game, and Jefferson can't go five seconds without talking.

"Seven-thirty to eight, reading again," Putt-Putt said. "Eight to eight-thirty, a special treat. But no more about that right now."

Everything was divided into hours and half hours with lots of reading. At the end we'd count our pages, have talking time, and then lights out and silence.

I clenched my hands behind my back. It would be OK.

"How many pages are we supposed to have read?" Rosie asked, stroking Pebbles who was nibbling at the cuff of her sweater.

"Just as many as you get read," Goldie said.

"Hey, Rosie," Jefferson called. "Pebbles is molting. Look at those big bald spots on his chest."

We peered at Pebbles, and Rosie began smoothing his chest fur, fluffing it up to cover the bare parts. "You just leave him alone, Jefferson Ames!"

"And leave Rosie alone, too, Jefferson," Goldie said. She opened her arms wide as if hugging us all, and her gold rings and bracelets flashed in the lights. "And now, dear Rabbits, let's get comfy in our sleeping bags for a happy reading time."

"Music on or off?" Putt-Putt asked.

We all yelled "On!"

"It's called a 'Fingl's Cave,'" Putt-Putt said. "If you listen, you may hear mermaids singing."

Pretty soon there was no sound at all in the cafeteria except the rustle of pages turning and the sweet voices of the mermaids. If you closed your eyes, you could imagine yourself on a beach with the surf beating on the sand. But of course if you closed your eyes, you couldn't read, so that didn't work too well. Besides, Tony Garcia was munching something that sounded like corn curls, which spoiled the effect, even though I pretended the snap-snap-snapping came from little sea creatures crackling in their shells.

By the time we stopped reading at seven, I was on page 11 of *The Phantom Tollbooth*.

"Do you like it?" Blake asked as we gathered in the middle of the floor for Quiet Ball.

"It's great," I said. "I hardly wanted to stop."

Blake nodded. "I know. That's how I get when I'm reading something good."

"Garfield's so funny," Sylvie told us, coming over and interrupting. "Look at his face here. Isn't that the funniest thing you ever saw?" She held her Garfield book so Blake could see it and I couldn't, and they were both laughing. I felt really out of it for a minute, but then Quiet Ball started, and right away we were all racing silently around the cafeteria.

Jefferson jumped on a table and yelled, "Here I am!" So he was out straight away.

64

"I guess you were right, Malcolm," he said.

It was fun. But it was nice at seven-thirty to get back to reading again. There was no music this time, and Mrs. Golden brought around a paper plate with celery sticks stuffed with peanut butter. We each took two, and Pebbles got the tops. I honestly don't think there's anything as cozy in the world as lying on a sleeping bag with your friends all around you, munching celery with peanut butter and reading a good book. Magic is right! But a cloud still hung on the edge of my mind, spreading and darkening like the shadow that stained the ceiling above the kitchen cabinets. I tried and tried to push it away, but clouds and shadows don't have anything to push on. It's the way it is when you're, say, in the mall shopping with a friend on Saturday morning and having a good time. But you know in the afternoon you have to go in to the doctor's office for your shots. And knowing those shots are coming spoils things. Sometimes you forget for a few minutes. And then you remember and you get scared all over again. I'd think about the silence and the dark coming, and something inside me would begin to shake. And I'd be reading and not understanding the words. And I'd have to go back and read the sentence all over again.

"Mark your places," Putt-Putt said. "It's surprise time. Girls, make room so the boys can sit next to you."

Naturally all the girls flurried to one side so there'd be room for the boys at the other end. It would have been nice to have made room for Blake beside me, but such things are just not possible. I guess not even for Sylvie Pedersen, who bunched herself up with the rest of the girls.

And then, through the cafeteria doors, came Goldie and Mr. Golden.

We all gasped. Goldie was wearing a long golden dress, and she had a sparkly golden band around her hair. I guess

65

Mr. Golden hadn't told her she looked like a ripe banana in *that* dress. He was just as fancy as she was in a dark red jacket and bow tie. Over his shoulder was a big accordion.

"Ladies and gentlemen Rabbits, may I present the Goldens," Putt-Putt said. Mr. Golden played a trill of notes on his accordion, and Mrs. Golden began to sing. We were all spellbound. Who would ever have guessed Goldie could sing like that?

Most of the songs I'd never heard before. One was about boys going off to war, and one about old people with nowhere to live, and one about a family leaving its homeland forever, the words so sad they made a lump come into your throat. But other songs were funny, about a frog who went a-courting, and about a guy whose name was Sue, so everybody thought he was a wimp, but he wasn't. As a finale we sang "There Was an Old Woman Who Swallowed a Fly," all of us together. We sounded so good that when we came to the end, Tina Semple whistled with her fingers in her mouth. I thought that was a much better way of getting attention than all her "Are you crazy's?" But Putt-Putt would never let her whistle like that in class.

"Aren't you glad we're Rabbits and we got to come tonight?" Claudia whispered. "Isn't it all fun?"

It really was.

We had more reading then and after that games again. We played Simon Says and Grandmother's Steps and King and Queen.

"Let's see now." Putt-Putt gazed around the room. "I think Blake will be King and . . ." I held my breath, hoping he'd choose me for Queen, hoping he wouldn't. "And Janey will be Queen," he said.

Oh no! Oh please! Sometimes I wonder how much Putt-Putt and other teachers know about our innermost thoughts.

"Great, Janey!" Claudia pushed me forward so Putt-Putt could put the eraser on my head. He had already put another one on Blake's.

"Queen!" Putt-Putt called first. That meant I should walk or run away from Blake, keeping the eraser on my head without touching it. If Blake tagged me, or if the eraser fell off, I'd lose my turn. To be King or Queen is really hard. Even so, everyone wants to be chosen.

Just when Blake almost caught up with me, Putt-Putt called "King," which meant we had to turn around fast, and Blake had to get away from me.

The boys were all cheering for the King, and the girls for the Queen, the way they always do. I heard Goldie call: "Keep your head up, Jane." Goldie likes this game because she says it's good for the posture. She also likes that we use erasers for crowns and not books, because "books are to be safely treasured, not put in places where they can fall and be damaged."

"Queen!" Putt-Putt called, and we turned again, and now I was the one being chased. I was going as quickly as I could, remembering not to let my feet turn out because already I'd heard someone horrible say "quack-quack," and I knew who that somebody horrible was, even though I couldn't look. I tilted my head back because my eraser was slipping forward on my newly washed and shiny hair. Blake was just one step behind.

"King," Mr. Puttinski shouted. Putt-Putt loves to do that at the last second. I turned fast, and Blake was reaching out with both arms to catch me, and I bumped right smack into him.

His eraser fell off. So did mine. I grabbed for it, even though you're not supposed to, and my fist clonked Blake right on the top of his nose.

"Wow! Great left hook!" Jefferson Ames shouted.

Blake yelped and jumped back, covering his nose with both hands. Right away his eyes filled with tears.

"Oh gosh. Oh, I'm sorry." I didn't know what to say, and then I said the worst thing I've ever said in my life. If only I'd kept quiet. If only I'd been too mortified to speak, which I almost was. But unfortunately the words spilled out. I think I'm accustomed to saying things like this to my little sisters, and for a second I forgot that this was Blake Conway—a boy—the boy I liked.

"Please don't cry, Blake," I said.

His teary eyes glared at me above the hand that covered his nose. "I am *not* crying," he said. "My eyes are watering." His voice sounded funny, all choked up, but it was probably because it had to come through his hand.

Then Goldie and Mr. Golden were beside us. "Let me have a look, Blake," Mr. Golden said. Blake took his cover-up hand away, and I saw that already his poor nose was turning red.

"I'm sorry, I'm sorry," I said again, sounding a bit choky myself. Mr. Golden touched Blake's nose.

"You're going to have a bump, but nothing serious. I've coached baseball and football enough to know a serious nose job when I see one. Let's go in the kitchen and get some ice."

And then suddenly Sylvie Pedersen was there, too, holding a box of Band-Aids and a little tube of cream. "I brought these," she said. "You can use them." Sylvie was looking all anxious, as if she were Blake's mother or at least his aunt—certainly someone very special.

"I don't think he's going to need a Band-Aid, Sylvie. But thank you," Goldie said.

I stood, desolate, as she and Mr. Golden led Blake to the kitchen.

"OK, everybody." Putt-Putt spoke in his normal, everyday cheery voice, which I knew was meant to let us know there was nothing to worry about.

"I guess we need a new King and Queen."

I guessed we did.

11

It was eleven-thirty, and we girl Rabbits were in the bathroom, teeth-brushing and changing into our pj's. Sylvie did look darling, tail and all. Actually, I thought we were all pretty cute, even Rosie, who had cream flannel pajamas that buttoned like a boy's. She was the only one of us who'd brought a robe, and she had enormous matching rabbit slippers in pale blue.

"I guess they're OK," she said, looking down at the slippers. "My mom got them for me specially. That's why I like them."

Sylvie looked down, too, and gave a little giggle.

"They're nice," I said, glaring at Sylvie and crossing my fingers behind my back. Actually the slippers were OK; it was just that they were so big—big enough so you could have put a real rabbit in each one and had room to spare.

"I wonder how Blake's nose is?" Sylvie said, watching

me in the mirror. "Honestly, I nearly died when you did that, Janey."

"She didn't mean to," Rosie said quickly, and Claudia added, "It was Putt-Putt's fault. He made Janey turn too quickly. Old Silly Putty! That's *dangerous*."

Sylvie leaned closer to the mirror and smeared a little Vaseline on her eyelashes.

"What's that for?" Rosie asked.

"It helps the lashes grow," Sylvie said in her superior way.

"Does it work for bosoms?" Claudia asked, all fake wide-eyed.

Betty Wu giggled. "Let's have some." She pretended to grab for the tube of Vaseline, but Sylvie frowned and dropped it into the little padded cosmetic bag that matched her pj's.

"Don't be dumb, Betty," she said. "There are exercises to make bosoms grow. I do them every night, but not here, of course."

"Wow, you really work at things, don't you?" Tina asked, and Sylvie shrugged.

"My mother says you're *never* too young to start building for the future."

"No kidding? Mine only tells me not to slouch and not to talk with my mouth full," Tina said.

I thought Tina looked really nice tonight. She had white pj's with little pink elephants all over them, elephants with trunks that probably walked kerplunks. *Oh, Blake. I wish I hadn't banged you on your nose!*

Sylvie had produced a tube of hand cream and was massaging it around her fingers.

"Is that to make your fingers grow?" Rosie asked, really interested.

Sylvie ignored her and looked at Tina. "That Jefferson

Ames is such a pain," she said. She was doing something odd now with her top lip, holding it at each side and tugging down on it.

"You should tell Putt-Putt to make him quit teasing you," she said. "Saying you have cooties and stuff like that."

Tina was brushing her teeth, and she had to spit foam before she could answer.

"He *knows* I don't have cooties." She wiped her mouth on a towel. "That was just an excuse."

Sylvie stopped tugging altogether. "What do you mean an excuse?"

"Well, if he thought I had cooties, he wouldn't have *kissed* me, would he?"

Bombshell! We all stared at Tina. Even Sylvie's mouth had dropped open in astonishment. Tina hummed a little tune and leaned into the mirror to examine a small zit on her forehead.

Sylvie was the first to recover her powers of speech. "*Kissed* you? Jefferson Ames?"

Tina pulled her hair forward so it covered the zit and nodded. "Well, he tried to anyway. I pulled away, and all he got was my chin."

"Your *chin*?" We were agog. Even a chin kiss sounded pretty terrific.

"You pulled away?" Claudia sounded astonished, and no wonder.

"But *where* did he kiss you?" Betty Wu asked.

Tina sighed. "I told you. On my chin. He was trying for somewhere better, but he didn't make it."

"She doesn't mean *that* kind of where," Sylvie said. "She means, where were you . . . geographically . . . when Jefferson Ames kissed you? *I* certainly didn't *see* him do it."

"You weren't there. It was in the third-grade classroom.

He was chasing me with the cootie catcher, and it was dark, and as soon as we got inside, he grabbed my arm and pulled me around, and that's when he did it." Tina paused for effect, and I must say the effect was fabulous. We all waited, hanging on for her next words. "If I hadn't pulled away, it would have landed right *here!*" She touched her mouth with her fingers and rolled her eyes. I have to admit she sounded exceptionally smug, and I don't blame her. She was probably the first one of us to be kissed by a boy. "He might have tried again, but Goldie called to us—to come out."

"Wow!" Claudia said. "That's really something, Tina. I told Janey before that I thought Jefferson liked you."

Tina grinned. "No kidding? When did you think that?"

But before Claudia could answer Sylvie said, "A kiss on the *chin* doesn't count."

"It does if none of us has anything else to count," I said.

"And a kiss anywhere's a kiss," Claudia added.

Sylvie gave her little, tinkly laugh. "From Jefferson Ames? With a cootie catcher?"

"I think he's pretty nice looking," I said, which might be true if you like tall, skinny boys who jump around and never shut up and if you don't mind someone who's rude and thinks insults are funny. Actually, it was pretty nice of *me* to stick up for him. He'd definitely been the one to "quack-quack" when I was Queen.

I sighed, remembering too well. If only Putt-Putt hadn't chosen me. If only that dumb eraser hadn't slipped.

All during the last reading time Blake had lain on his sleeping bag with a cold pack on his nose. Goldie had fixed it for him with ice cubes in a plastic bag. Every time he moved we could hear the cubes rattle.

Afterward, when we'd stopped reading and sat eating

our snacks, all I could see of him were his eyes peering over the big plastic balloon of melted ice. I'd planned on sharing my raisins and telling him how far I'd gotten in *The Phantom Tollbooth,* but I didn't dare. Maybe I wouldn't have dared anyway. But I might have. Maybe. Even the maybe had vanished. Just before we came in the bathroom, Goldie had treated us all to frozen yogurts that she'd stored in the refrigerator, and Blake had held his ice pack with one hand and slurped his frozen yogurt with the other. Poor Blake!

I washed with my Wild Flower soap now and stared at myself in the mirror. Imagine if it had been Blake Conway who'd kissed my chin in the third-grade classroom! I knew one thing. I'd never have washed my chin again!

"Knock! Knock!" Goldie opened the bathroom door and sniffed. "My, it smells good in here. 'Evening in Paris and Ashes of Roses,' as we would have said when I was young. Well, the time has come for all of us to crawl into our sleeping bags. We have pages to count and then fifteen minutes till lights out."

I folded my towel and tried to smile reassuringly at Claudia. Oh, man! OK. Here it was.

My smile was supposed to show Claudia how brave I was, how unscared. What a lie! Inside, my stomach was starting to quease up again.

Goldie held the door for us, and there were Putt-Putt and Mr. Golden and the six guys all coming out of the boys' bathroom. There was Blake. The part of him I noticed first was his nose, shining red as the sun.

I swallowed. "Is it . . . does it hurt a lot, Blake?"

"Not that much," he said and turned away. What had happened to all that good talk about *The Dune Story Book?*

I'd probably never in all my life know if Paul was able to save the galaxy from the evil emperor.

Jefferson Ames was towering as usual over all the other boys. I tried not to stare at him, but I couldn't help it, and I knew all the other girls were looking, too. He'd changed. He was the first sixth-grade boy we knew who'd kissed a sixth-grade girl. There was a kind of awe in that.

"Criminy, look at all those far-out pajamas," he said and pointed to Sylvie, who was gliding along in her pink bunny outfit, her eyelashes shining and her top lip looking good, too, though I hadn't quite figured out what the tugging had done for it. Jefferson began whistling, "Here comes Peter Cottontail, hopping down the bunny trail," in time with Sylvie's steps.

"Oh, honestly, Jefferson!" Sylvie said in a very aggravated voice. I knew this wasn't the kind of pj attention she'd been hoping for.

Jefferson spotted Rosie's slippers and stopped whistling. "Hey, Rosie! Watch out you don't trip on your ears."

"Watch out someone doesn't poke you in the eye," I said, and Jefferson cringed back. "Oh oh. She's dangerous. First the nose, then the eye—!"

Jefferson Ames really is a pain. It's so rude to pass remarks like this. And I actually don't think he's that nice looking. I'd been almost envying Tina her experience, but then I thought how awful it would be to remember your first kiss for the rest of your life and have to remember you got it from Jefferson Ames.

Malcolm was edging toward Claudia. "I didn't know you were on the Dodgers," he said. "Where do you play?"

Claudia had a startled look. I guess she and I are always startled if Blake or Malcolm speaks to us. It hasn't happened that often. "Er . . . ah . . . in Dodger Stadium," she said.

"No. I mean, are you a pitcher or a catcher or what?"

"She's a Fairfielder," Jefferson yelled. "Get it? Claudia Fairfield?"

"You forgot something, though." Malcolm whipped off his Dodger cap and tossed it sideways to Claudia.

Claudia, who is not intensely coordinated, missed it, and Sylvie Pedersen caught it instead.

She dropped it fast. "Oh, grimy-gross," she said. "It's all sweaty and everything!"

Claudia picked the cap up and put it on. It came all the way over her eyes, so she had to push it back. Under the peak her face was pink, but I don't think anybody noticed. They were all too busy staring at Malcolm.

"Gee, Malcolm, you sure look different," Betty Wu said.

He sure did. He had the bushiest hair I'd ever seen, curly as a poodle's and flat on top where the cap had nested for about a million years.

"Would you like it back now?" Claudia asked.

Malcolm nodded toward the pile of stuff beside his sleeping bag. "That's OK. I've got a spare. You know, the Dodgers might do OK this year. I've been watching some of their training sessions on TV."

"Oh, ah, that's good," Claudia said. I could tell all this was beyond her wildest dreams.

Rosie was scuffling along behind me. She looked as if she were about to cry.

I waited for her to catch up and whispered, "Don't worry about stupid old Jefferson Ames. He's probably wishing he'd thought of getting bunny slippers himself."

"It's not that," Rosie said.

"Well, what's the matter?"

76

"Nothing."

"Is it . . . are you worried about Pebbles?"

Rosie nodded. "That, too. He's just lying in his box, not moving or anything. And he was making that little cheeping noise."

"Well, maybe he's tired."

"Maybe." Every bit of Rosie seemed to droop. Even the bunny ears on her slippers hung limp.

"Jane?" she whispered.

"Yes?" I'd never heard anyone sound so totally sad. "Yes?" I said again. "What's the matter?"

"I . . . I can't . . ." She stopped and shook her head.

We were way back of everybody now, standing by ourselves.

"Is it—something about your grandfather?" I asked.

Rosie's eyes met mine, and I saw she was crying. "No. Well, yes. Sort of . . ."

"Is it because . . . well, because he's going blind?"

"Oh, I shouldn't have said anything. Forget it. Forget it please, Jane."

And then she was sliding along in the big slippers, as fast as she could go, heading for the ring of sleeping bags.

I walked slowly behind her. Poor Rosie! I wouldn't know what else to say to her even if I did catch up, and I was in no hurry to get into my sleeping bag and have the night begin.

12

Goldie stood in the floor space between the sleeping bags and smiled her golden smile. "Rabbits, on this one night we have a total of 300 pages read."

We were all sitting up, waiting for her announcement, and when she and Mr. Golden and Putt-Putt applauded, we joined in. Tina gave her finger whistle, and some of the kids tried to copy her, but they weren't very good.

Claudia arranged Malcolm's cap, which she was wearing, pushing it back so it wouldn't slip down and suffocate her. "Are you going to sleep in that?" I asked.

Claudia smiled. "For sure!"

We looked across at Malcolm, who was wearing his spare. "It's really nice to know he isn't bald," Claudia said, and smiled again.

"What's happening with the balloons, Mr. Puttinski?" Chip Wu asked.

"We'll have the balloon fiesta tomorrow morning before we leave," Putt-Putt said.

"And they'll drift toward heaven," Goldie added. "Each one carrying your name . . . your name and the title of the wonderful book you read on the night of the sixth-grade sleepover at Fred Barrington School." Goldie spoke in the hushed voice she always uses when she talks about books—almost holy. And Mr. Golden was looking at her as if she were holy, too.

Jefferson Ames interrupted the holy quiet. "What's for breakfast?"

Goldie sighed. "I was talking about food for the soul. But rest assured, there'll be lots of good things." She checked her watch and glanced at Putt-Putt.

"I'll get the lights," Putt-Putt said. He waited till Goldie and Mr. Golden wriggled into their sleeping bags and then went across to the light switch.

"Everybody ready?"

We squirmed down, and there was a click as the lights went off.

Oh, it was dark! I blinked and held onto the top of my sleeping bag, getting my eyes used to the change, telling my eyes to tell my stomach and all the other parts of me that were quivering that it was really OK.

"Janey?" Claudia's hand came sneaking across to touch mine that was twitching nervously now like some kind of frightened beached fish.

"It's all right," I whispered. But it wasn't. Claudia's fingers curled tightly around mine.

I raised my head a little. The light from the bathroom doors slanted across the bottom of my sleeping bag, narrowing beyond me into darkness. The night lights Dad had brought from home were small squares, no more than yellow windows in dollhouses. From floor level the kitchen counter was a block wall that hid everything behind it.

Oh, help! I tried not to let my breath get raggedy, but I could feel my chest starting to hurt.

And then Putt-Putt began to shut the bathroom doors.

I sat straight up. "Hey!" I said. "Don't do that!"

"I'm just closing them a little. The light's right in Malcolm's face."

"Malcolm can move then," Claudia said. "We want the doors open."

"What's the matter, scaredy-cat?" That was Jefferson Ames, of course, sly as a troll. "Are you scared of the dark, babykins Claudia?"

"Well, I know *you're* not, Jefferson Ames," Claudia said. "I know *you* like it for kissing!"

All the guys began whistling and yelling stuff like "Who've you been kissing, Jefferson?" and thumping their hands on the wooden floor. The noise made Jefferson shut up all right.

"Don't worry about me," Malcolm said when the teasing stopped. "I've got my cap down over my eyes. I couldn't see a searchlight if it was right on me. These caps have amazing density."

So Putt-Putt left the doors open, and Claudia and I held hands, out of sight between our two bags.

"So what will we talk about?" Putt-Putt asked. I saw his shadowy outline settle into his sleeping bag, punch up his pillow. "We've got ten minutes."

"Ghost stories," Tony Garcia said. "I know some good ones."

"Riddles." That was Malcolm.

"Let's have riddles," I called out.

"Why was the cannibal king sick to his stomach?"

None of us could guess.

"Because he was fed up with people."

"Oh revolto! Oh barf city!"

"What did the kitty-cat say when the three mice went by on their skateboards?" That was Betty Wu. She didn't wait for us to guess. "He said, 'Oh boy. Meals on wheels.' "

We all laughed. "That's pretty good," Malcolm said. I guess he considers himself a riddle expert. I really like them, too. When you laugh, you forget the bad things.

I was glad I still had *The Best Christmas Pageant Ever* for later. When I wouldn't be in the cafeteria.

"Mr. Puttinski?" Rosie was sitting up in her bag next to mine. "May I go and say good night to Pebbles one more time?"

"I don't think he wants to be disturbed, Rosie," Putt-Putt said. "Last time I checked he was fast asleep."

Rosie lay down again. She was calling, "Here, Pebbles, here, Pebbles," the way you'd beg a dog to come, very, very softly. She clicked her fingers in his direction, but Pebbles didn't come.

We spent a long time calling our good nights. Flashlight beams sliced the dark, across sleeping bags, reflecting the pale colors of the balloons.

"Good night, Malcolm."

"Good night, Chip and Betty."

"Good night, Mrs. Golden."

"Good night, Mr. Golden."

I tried multiplying how many good nights there would be with twelve Rabbits and three adults, but my math isn't that good. I did know Blake hadn't said good night to me.

"Good night, Jane." Oh goodness, there he was.

"Good night, Blake."

I waited, hoping and hoping he'd say something else, and he did. "My nose doesn't hurt anymore."

"Oh, oh good."

"Well it *looks* just terrible!" Sylvie Pedersen's voice was super sweet and concerned.

"No it doesn't," Claudia said. "It doesn't look bad at all."

I lay, ringed in the almost dark, listening to the little whispers, the sighs, the rustles, the breathings. There was a small crunching, the kind that's trying to be quiet, slow, and apologetic. Goldie! Munching celery in bed! I remembered that she hadn't brought a snack and that she hadn't eaten any of her own frozen yogurt. Did she always eat celery at night? Her teeth were probably better than anyone's.

The crunching stopped. A tiny edge of moonlight crept through the slatted blinds, high on the cafeteria wall. I could see one small star. Claudia's hand slackened and fell away from mine.

"Claudia?"

She didn't answer.

I felt under my pillow for my flashlight, turned it on, and sent its shine around the cafeteria. No one spoke. No one moved. The beam poked the top corners of the ceiling. When I jerked it away, something slithered in the new dark place I'd just left. I shone the light back quickly. There was nothing. But now I'd left something behind in the last place— something hidden, humped, horrible.

I bit hard on my lips. *Don't call out, Jane. Don't cry.* I shut off the flashlight and made myself close my eyes. When you close your eyes, you don't see the blackness, so in a way it's better. But if something should pounce, you wouldn't see it coming. My eyelids jerked open. Kerplunk, kerplunk, kerplunk. How could my heart make so much sound and nobody waken?

Too soon yet to do what I had to do. Five minutes more.

I could stand the dark for five more minutes, couldn't I? Then I'd be certain everyone was asleep. I'd count to a hundred.

One hippopotamus, two hippopotamuses. I'd count to fifty.

Was Blake asleep? I'd think about Blake. He'd called me Jane, not Janey. That was nice. Maybe he magically knew I liked Jane better. Thinking about Blake didn't keep the terror away either.

Someone moved. Someone got up, glided through the darkness. I lay stiff and rigid. The person crossed through the cone of light. It was Jefferson Ames, tall and skinny and walking very quietly. Going where? He wasn't about to kiss Tina again, was he? She'd waken, think there was a bug on her face, scream, and have a conniption.

What was he doing? He was untying the strings of the balloons, letting them float free to bob soundlessly against the ceiling.

I should yell, tell him to stop. But then everyone would be awake, and I'd have to wait some more.

One balloon drifted over his head as he went to where Tina slept. I couldn't see what he was doing, but in a minute I knew. Now the balloon hovered over her. He'd tied it to something—to her wrist maybe, or one of her fingers. It was like X marks the treasure. I watched Jefferson as he edged back and into his own sleeping bag.

How weird! I lay, pondering. He must like her! That's what it meant when you teased a girl all the time, and kissed her, and tied a balloon over her head.

Watching Jefferson had made me almost forget the dark, but not all the way. Now it was so silent again. Was Jefferson asleep, too? I'd have to wait some more.

Thirty hippopotamuses, thirty-one hippopotamuses . . .

Soon. One part of my mind kept counting. The other part

went over exactly what I had to do. I'd get up, take my sleeping bag and my pack that had my books and my alarm clock, and I'd go quietly to the bathroom. There would be no way to spread out on the floor because someone could come in and see me. I'd go to the stall farthest away from the door, put the toilet seat down, wrap the sleeping bag around me, and sit there till morning. If Goldie only knew how many more pages she could add onto my total count! And I'd set my alarm, just in case I dropped off to sleep sitting up. But I'd better not, because what if I toppled over and made a big commotion? Then, in WHO, WHAT, WHERE, WHEN, AND WHY they'd *really* be able to write "Janey Winston fell into the toilet." It wouldn't happen, though, because I had *The Best Christmas Pageant Ever* to make me laugh and keep me awake. And it would be so nice and bright in there, so safe and shining white.

Three more hippopotamuses and I could go.

And then I felt a movement beside me, a sneaky kind of rustling. I moved only my eyes. Rosie!

She crawled out of her sleeping bag, and I thought, *She's going to check on Pebbles again. Or she's going to get him and bring him over here.*

I kept my eyes closed. *Whatever you're going to do, Rosie, do it fast and then go back to sleep.* I could have howled. She was still awake, and that meant I'd have to wait some more, and I didn't know if I could stand it, with the dark building inside of me, swelling like some horrible sore filled with yuk and about to burst.

I squinted through half-closed eyes. *Hurry, Rosie! Get him, and then both of you go to sleep.* Please. Please.

In the shaft of light from the doors, I saw her put on her robe and pick up her bunny slippers and her book bag.

Where was she going? Carefully, on bare, silent feet, Rosie headed for the bathroom.

13

The light from one door was suddenly cut off, so there was only a single narrow sliver and the pale gleam of the dollhouse windows close to the floor. No! No!

No more hippopotamuses! No more lying here, shaking like a frightened rabbit!

I unzipped my sleeping bag and fumbled my way out. The lining pulled in a tangle around my feet, and I kicked it free. *Let me out of here, out of the dark.*

I ran to the bathroom and jerked open the door. Light! Shadowless, hard, wonderful light! I took a deep breath. It was as if I'd been drowning and had found air.

One of the stall doors was closed.

It was a minute or so before I could move. Then I tapped on the door. "Rosie? It's Jane."

She didn't answer.

"Rosie?"

There was no sound at all.

I pushed against the door panel, but it was locked. When

I bent down, I could see the two enormous slippers with Rosie's feet inside them.

"Open the door, Rosemary. I want to talk to you."

Now I was getting scared. Was she sick? I'd better get Goldie. Something was wrong.

Then the bolt cracked back, and there was Rosie. I stared past her. She had the toilet seat lowered, the way I'd planned to do. Her backpack was on the floor, and she was holding *Julie of the Wolves*, which I'd seen her reading earlier tonight.

"You're still *reading*?" I whispered.

She nodded, and I saw that her eyes were blobbed with tears.

"But . . . but why? I mean, why *now*?"

Rosie stood to one side. "Come in."

There was hardly any room. I leaned against the cold, written-over wall. It didn't matter how many times they painted that bathroom wall, it always got written on again . . . boys' names inside hearts, boys' and girls' names together inside hearts. Rosie sat down on the closed seat.

"I don't get it," I whispered. "Can't you sleep? Or . . .?" I had this sudden, astonishing thought. "Are you . . . scared of the dark?"

Rosie shook her head. "Not really."

"You were just reading?" I asked.

"Trying to."

"I still don't get it." I put one foot on top of the other, shivering and wishing that I had my little pink and white ballet slippers.

Rosie's voice was so low that I could scarcely hear her. "I don't know *how* to read very well, Jane. It takes me ten times as long as the rest of you. And even *then* I don't understand half of it. Do you know how much I read tonight?"

I shook my head, speechless.

"Two pages." Rosie was all watery-eyed, her nose dripping, her stringy hair hanging stringy against her blotchy cheeks. She was the saddest thing I'd ever seen.

"Oh please," I said, just the way I'd said to Blake. "Please don't cry."

She pulled off a piece of toilet paper, wiped her eyes, and blew her nose.

None of this made sense to me. "I thought you told Goldie you read twenty-three pages tonight," I said. "I saw her write it down."

"I'd *turned* twenty-three pages. That doesn't mean I'd read them. Goldie looked over my shoulder and just figured I'd read that many. I knew she would. I've used that trick before."

"But . . . but what about *The Day of the Jackal?* What about all those books you read to your grandfather?"

"I get the tapes out of the library. I play one for him, and I try to follow along in the book. But I'm always lost."

I edged down onto the floor.

"Here." Rosie took off her rabbit slippers and put them on my feet. They felt so warm and heavenly.

"You can't read at *all?*" I was totally stunned. "But how can you be in the sixth grade and not be able to read?"

"I can read *One Fish Two Fish* and *Goodnight Moon.* Books like that. Not the hard ones."

"But . . . the Rabbit Club?"

"I told Goldie I'd read twelve books this month. It was true. I'd read *Zoo Babies* and *Cat in the Hat* . . . twelve of them. Then I told her the stories of *Day of the Jackal* and all the others I'd listened to with my grandfather."

"You told Goldie *lies*?"

"I did *not*." Rosie's eyes glittered. "I would *never* tell Goldie lies. I like her. She's nice to me. Anyway, my mom signed that I read twelve books. She didn't lie either. I told her I'd read twelve, so she signed. She didn't ask which ones."

"Your mom doesn't know? I mean, that you can't . . . that you're not a very good reader?"

"She doesn't have time to know. She works two jobs, and sometimes on Saturdays, too. All she has time for is keeping Grandpa and me and herself fed and getting the rent paid."

"Oh." I didn't want to ask where Rosie's father was or anything about him.

"Mom knows I *used* to read," Rosie said. "Because we used to read together, back in the second grade. When things were different." She sat with her elbows on her knees and her chin in her hands. Poor Rosie!

"I don't understand why you decided to try for the Rabbit Club, though," I said. "I mean, why did you want to be in with the best readers? And having to keep up and stuff?"

Rosie blinked at me. "A Rabbit is a friend to every other Rabbit," she said. "Rule Number 6. It was one way to get to have friends. I don't seem to be able to in ordinary ways."

Oh crumbs and double crumbs! I couldn't even *look* at her, I felt so bad.

I said, "Claudia and I will help you. You can come to my house, and we'll all read. I taught Rachel how . . . I mean, she can read a bit, and she's only six. We'll start with the easy books and work up and . . ." I grabbed her arm. "Goldie *tutors* reading at some church every Saturday. You could go to *her*."

"No," Rosie said. "Then she'd know. They'd all know."

"Who cares? It's nothing to be ashamed of. Look, it's only going to get worse and worse if you don't ask for help. Honest. It will build and build . . . and . . ." I was listening to myself telling Rosie this, and here I was with a gigantic problem of my own that I didn't want anybody to know. "It's going to get worse if you don't ask for help," I'd told her. So what about me?

"You can't keep hiding in the bathroom for the rest of your life," I said, trying to be funny. But it wasn't funny for me either.

"Well, anyway, I have to read these twenty-three pages tonight." Rosie gave a funny little gulp, and I could see the tears starting again. "The numbers are going up to heaven tomorrow. Goldie said."

We looked at each other for a long time.

"OK." I scrambled up. "I'll help you. We'll read it together. But first I've got to get my sleeping bag and my slippers before I freeze to death. I'll be back."

"You don't have to, Jane. I mean, you don't want to stay in here all night."

"I was planning to anyway," I said. "I'm afraid of the dark."

Rosie didn't seem surprised. "I am a bit, too. My grandfather says everyone is. It's because you don't know what's there. Did you know when you're going blind they have people who come to explain to you how to handle the darkness that's coming? Maybe you could talk to one of them."

"I know a pretty good guy myself," I said. "His name's Doctor Bishop. I might go see him again."

I gave Rosie back her slippers. "Should I bring my sleeping bag, too?" I asked. "We could sit on one and put the other one over us."

"OK. Sure."

I spread the bathroom door wide so I'd have light and padded back into the cafeteria. Claudia had turned over, and her cap was on the floor. I picked it up and set it on her stomach. Then I knelt beside the bunched-up lining of my sleeping bag.

Something went "eek, eek, eek."

I pulled my hands away fast.

"Eek, eek, peep, peep" . . . right inside the lining. Something was in there, something alive.

"Eek!" I screamed at the top of my lungs. "Eek!"

14

It was worse than the night I'd screamed in Claudia's house, because here there were more people to hear me. Everyone seemed to come awake at once.

"Who's screaming? What is it?" That was Putt-Putt. A flashlight beam probed toward me. "Janey?"

Goldie stumbled in my direction. "Put the lights on, Bertrand. Quick!"

But before anyone could do anything, the lights *were* on, and I saw Rosie with her hand on the switch. "Jane? Jane, what happened?"

Claudia crawled toward me, her sleeping bag tangled around her legs. From somewhere far away I heard Tina Semple yelling, "Am I crazy or is there a balloon tied to me somewhere?"

I stared at the lining of my sleeping bag. Inside it something moved—something wet. A black stain spread across the pale yellow flannel.

"Stand back!" Putt-Putt picked up the lining, opened it, dropped it on the sleeping bag, and stood back himself.

"Eeeek, eek, eek!"

In the middle of the opened lining was a wet patch, and in the middle of it was Pebbles and a squirming mess of little, pink bald things.

"Well, I'll be . . ." Putt-Putt said. "Rabbit babies!"

We all crowded around, looking down.

"*That's* what was the matter with him," Goldie said.

"With her, you mean," Putt-Putt corrected. "But I don't . . ." He stopped and grinned. "Remember the day Macho Rabbit came to visit? We thought he and Pebbles got to be good buddies pretty fast."

"They got to be *real* good buddies!" Mr. Golden said.

Rosie got down on her knees beside the nest, stroking Pebbles's fur. "Oh, they're so pretty, Pebbles. You are so clever!"

"I see six," Blake counted.

"Seven," Rosie said. "There's one under there."

Goldie found a cardboard box in the kitchen and padded it with a towel, and Putt-Putt lifted the tiny rabbits into it, one by one. Their eyes were tight closed, and they made this funny squeaking sound. Pebbles hopped in beside them, and the babies began right away to nurse, feeling around her blindly, butting her with their little heads. They crawled on top of one another, tunneled under one another, wandered off in the wrong direction.

Rosie pointed to the littlest one of all. "Oh, Mr. Puttinski! Could I have this one?"

"We'll see, Rosie. We're not about to start making decisions at one-thirty in the morning." Putt-Putt yawned. "Where were you anyway, Janey, when Pebbles got in your sleeping bag?"

"In the bathroom. I'm sorry I screamed."

"I'd have screamed, *too*," Claudia said. "Imagine if you'd put your *feet* in!"

Everyone groaned, "Oh gross. Oh mucky!" and pretended to throw up.

"We'll have to read what to do with baby rabbits, and how long they stay with their mother," Goldie said happily. "No problem. We can find everything about everything in books!"

"Pebbles is a boy and he's a mother," Jefferson Ames said. "That's scary. I didn't *know* that could happen."

"Oh, you're so dumb, Jefferson." Tina sounded embarrassed. I would have been, too, if I liked a boy who was that dumb.

"But can I have *this* one?" Rosie begged. I remembered how she always held Pebbles, who was her friend, who was soft and warm and comforting.

"Later we'll make out papers for the babies and see who wants to adopt one," Putt-Putt said. "Meantime . . . mother and children seem to be doing fine. So why don't we all get back in our sleeping bags for the rest of the night? Can you do without your lining, Janey?"

I nodded. "Sure."

It was Goldie who said, "You must have been in the bathroom rather a long time, Jane."

"She was talking to me," Rosie said.

"We were talking to each other," I corrected.

"Oh." Goldie looked at us both with her wise, golden eyes . . . eyes that had seen a lot of kids and read a lot of truths in a lot of books. "Well, I like to talk, too. And to listen," she said. "Remember that."

"I'll remember," Rosie said, so seriously that I knew she meant it.

Goldie gave us each a hug and waited while we wriggled into our sleeping bags.

"Could we keep the lights on for the rest of the night, Mrs. Golden?" I whispered.

Goldie smiled. "Poor Jane. You did get quite a fright."

"It's not that," I said. "I'm . . . I'm afraid of the dark. I have been for as long as I can remember." It was such a relief to say the words out loud. I felt light and hollow inside.

Goldie smoothed back my hair. "I understand, honey." She raised her voice. "Does anybody mind if we keep the lights on?"

"No."

"We want to be able to see Pebbles, anyway," Rosie said.

So the lights stayed lit all night after all.

I drifted into sleep, and the thing that wakened me was the click of the switch turning the lights off. I swear, that sound would waken me if I were half dead.

I sat up fast. It was morning already, with sun coming through the high blinds, filling the cafeteria with its silver-pink glow. Some of the kids were up and dressed, and most of the sleeping bags were empty. A crowd clustered around Pebbles's box.

"We've given them all names," Rosie said as I went to look. "Mine is called Julie." She slanted a meaningful glance in my direction, and I knew she was remembering last night and *Julie of the Wolves*. I have a feeling that Rosie and I are going to exchange lots of meaningful looks in the future, the way Claudia and I do. The way you do with your best friends.

We had oranges and little boxes of cereal and delicious date-nut bread for breakfast. I was just finishing my second box of wheat crunchies when I looked up and saw Blake beside me. His nose had simmered down to a delicate shell pink.

"Hi," he said and handed me a card with a hole punched in it. There was a rabbit sticker in the corner and the words:

FRED BARRINGTON ELEMENTARY SCHOOL,
PASADENA, CALIFORNIA 91106.
At our sixth-grade sleepover on March 20, 1987,

I read _____ pages of _____

Signed: _____ Rabbit Reading Club

"We tie these to the balloons." Blake held out his Day-Glo pen. "Do you want to use this?"

"Oh thanks." I began filling the blanks on the card, and then Blake said, "You can keep the pen if you like." He was pinker than ever.

"Really? Thanks. It's a pretty nice pen." I couldn't believe this! Blake! Giving me a gift! Just wait till I told Claudia and Rosie!

Then Putt-Putt called us to come get our balloons. Tina still had the red one tied to her wrist, and Jefferson Ames reached around the whole bunch and got the other red one for himself. It seemed very meaningful.

I took a yellow one, and Sylvie took a blue.

"Look how pretty this one is," she said, smiling and turning the balloon so the light trapped itself inside, like the sun in the sky. "Isn't blue just your favorite, all-time color?" she asked Blake.

I told myself it didn't matter what color Blake took. I mean, boys probably don't pay attention to stuff like that—not boys like Blake. It wasn't meaningful at all. I held tight to the Day-Glo pen, which I'd clipped in the pocket of my corduroys.

Blake looked at me sort of shyly. Then, wonder of wonders, he picked the other yellow balloon.

We all stood on the steps of Fred Barrington Elementary with Pebbles and her babies in the box beside us. Each of us held a balloon with the card attached. I saw right away that Rosie had no card tied to hers. *Nice Rosie*, I thought. *She's making sure no lies of hers go up to heaven.*

"At the count of three," Goldie said. "One, two, three."

We let go of the strings, and the balloons rose in a rainbow of color against the pale wash of sky.

I wondered who'd find mine—if he or she would go out and get *The Phantom Tollbooth* and read it, too, and send me a letter. It was almost like spreading the news of books across the width of the world.

When I shaded my eyes, I saw that the two yellow balloons were drifting together, their strings tangled. *Mine and Blake's,* I thought, *holding hands.* It seemed very apropos.